THE UNIQUE MAGAZINE
SUMMER 1991

ISSN 0898-5073
Art by Bob Walters

Weird Tales® is published 4 times a year by Terminus Publishing Co., Inc., PO Box 13418,
Philadelphia PA 19101-3418 (4426 Larchwood Ave., Philadelphia PA 19104-3916). 2nd Class Postage
paid at Philadelphia PA & additional mailing offices. Single copies, $4.95. Subscriptions: 4 issues
(one year) $16.00 in U.S.A. & possessions; $20.00 in Canada & Mexico, $22.00 elsewhere, in U.S.
funds. Publisher is not responsible for loss of manuscripts, although publisher will take reasonable
care of them. Postmaster: send address changes to *Weird Tales*®, PO Box 13418, Philadelphia PA
19101-3418. Copyright © 1991 by Terminus Publishing Co., Inc.; all rights reserved; reproduction
prohibited without prior permission. Typeset, printed, & bound in the United States of America.
Weird Tales® is a registered trademark owned by Weird Tales, Limited.

THE EYRIE

In this, the 301st issue of *Weird Tales*®, we are proud to honor one of Great Britain's most distinguished horror writers. Ramsey Campbell has been with us for some time now. His first story, distinctly in the mode of H.P. Lovecraft, appeared in an Arkham House anthology in 1962 when he was sixteen years old. His first book, *The Inhabitant of the Lake and Less Welcome Tenants*, was published by Arkham House two years later. In the intervening years he has long since outgrown being a prodigy, broken away from Lovecraft, and established himself as the sole purveyor of his own distinctively subtle brand of horror fiction. His most recent novel, as of this writing, is *Ancient Images* (Tor).

We are also proud to offer congratulations to Ian R. MacLeod, whose novelet, "1/72nd Scale" (first published in *Weird Tales*® 298) is a finalist for the Nebula Award, the first story from our pages to be so honored. Whether it wins or not will be old news by the time you read our next issue, but we won't know until after this one is in press. So read it first in *Locus*; we'll keep you informed in any case.

A Few More Words About Reprints: We start this Eyrie with a letter from a slightly irate **Joe D. Zakem,** who writes:

I was pleased to see that Jonathan Carroll was chosen as the subject of one of your special issues, since he is one of my favorite contemporary writers. At least two of the Carroll stories in Number 299, however, appear to be reprints — "Postgraduate" was in Penthouse *several years back and "The Panic Hand" appeared in* Interzone 33, *which was dated January/February 1990. While I find nothing wrong with using previously published stories, especially work which may be unfamiliar to many of your readers, I do think you should indicate that the stories were originally printed elsewhere. I also wonder whether the other two Carroll stories in Number 299 were reprints or originals to* Weird Tales®.

We think we should be a little more open about it too, and apologize for failing to indicate, for example, that the original version of Robert Bloch's story, "Beetles," in issue 300 was a reprint from *Weird Tales* for December 1938. We reprinted it as an interesting contrast to the "Beetles" screenplay in the same issue.

As for the Carroll stories, we actually mentioned the reprint from *Penthouse* in the Eyrie of issue 298, where there is a more extended discussion of our reprint policy. We *will* continue to reprint stories from obscure sources when the occasion warrants, particularly by featured authors — and let's face it, for all *Penthouse* has a huge initial circulation, few people and fewer institutions save such magazines, so a 1978 issue is obscure indeed — and in a more general way, we will buy first North American serial rights to stories which have been published abroad. Technically, these are not reprints.

Carroll's "Tired Angel" came from a foreign source, the British magazine *Fear,* as did Ian Watson's "In Her Shoes" in issue 298. "My Zoondel" previously appeared in German, but not in English. Ray Bradbury's two poems in issue 300 are reprints from an out-of-print collection.

We admit we've sometimes been remiss in acknowledging this, but otherwise we have not broken our own reprint rules, or even bent them very much. "Beetles" (the story) will probably be our only reprint from the back-pages of *Weird Tales*® itself. Already there are many fine anthologies from the pages of the old magazine. We particularly recommend *Weird Tales: The Magazine that Never Dies* edited by Marvin Kaye (Nelson Doubleday) and *Weird Tales: 32 Unearthed Terrors* edited by Robert Weinberg (Bonanza Books).

Have You Noticed? Horror fiction seems to be undergoing one of its periodic identity crises of late. Reader **K. Newton** comments that he's just beginning to read Lovecraft, and commends *Weird Tales*® for being "the only magazine that continues to publish high quality Mythos-type fiction." He continues:

The newer magazines (i.e. Cemetery Dance; New Blood*) seem to be trying to change the concept of horror and make it more of a blood-and-guts, mystery--suspense, hard-boiled private-eye, gritty detective-vs-serial-killer, psycho killer . . .*

Publisher:
George H. Scithers

Editor:
Darrell Schweitzer

Managing Editor:
Carol Adams

Assistant Editors:
Leslie Smith, Dainis Bisenieks, Diane Weinstein, Michael W. Betancourt, & Don Keller

Circulation Manager:
Richard Kabakjian

Computer Consultant:
David J. Williams III

Of Counsel:
Yale F. Edeiken

Typesetter:
Campus Copy Center

Printer & Soft-Cover Binder:
Malloy Lithographing, Inc.

Hard-Cover Binder:
Hoster Bindery, Inc.

Mailing:
Unit Packaging Corporation

Manuscript Submissions:

Yes; we read unsolicited submissions — if they are in standard manuscript format. Editors survive only by insisting on a few Rules: each submission must include a return envelope with your address and enough postage to bring the manuscript back to you. If it's cheaper to have us discard the manuscript if not bought, tell us so, but include a business-letter-size envelope with your address and postage so we may send you our comments. Affix postage to envelope; don't send loose stamps.

Proper manuscript format is discussed in many reference works. Some of us have even written one: *On Writing Science Fiction: the Editors Strike Back!* by Scithers, Schweitzer, & Ford; $19.50 in hardcovers, from Owlswick Press, P.O. Box 8243, Philadelphia PA 19101-8243. Another excellent work from the same publisher is Barry B. Longyear's *Science-Fiction Writer's Workshop:* $9.50 in trade paperback. These prices include shipping and handling; in Pennsylvania, please include 6% sales tax.

We cannot be responsible for manuscripts in transit or in our hands; you **must** keep a copy of every manuscript you send out, and you **must** put your name and address on the first page of every manuscript. Please: no padded envelopes, folders, or binders; and no registered or certified mail.

in other words, demystify and dehumanize the horror tale. And, now that I think of it, I don't think "change" is the correct word; I believe that this new direction is the result of . . . lack of imagination. The "new" horror tale is horrific, yes — how can up close, "in the mind's eye" narratives exploring the motivations of murderers and molesters and other social deviants not be? — but it leaves out the one important element of the truly great horror tale: the imagination; the fact that the imaginative horror remains in one's mind long after the tale is told; that it touches and perhaps sheds light upon those hidden parts of the brain where dark thoughts gather; that it stimulates and invigorates the mind, stirs up the creative solution, the pea soup of consciousness . . . the imagination.

Without quite so much rhetoric, we have to agree.

Reader **W.F. Poynter** of Santa Rosa, CA adds:

. . . just what is "weird"? Is it fantasy, horror, scary tragedy? Is it bloody, splattery, violence, drugs, weapons? I think the area is wide open, and you declare you want this. But please lay off the TV specials and the New York Times *penchant for violence, drugs, blood, vomit, and shoot-em-ups.*

Indeed, we have noticed the trend, not only in magazines like *Cemetery Dance* but in the novels of best-selling "horror" writers, to blend horror fiction with crime fiction, producing what is sometimes called "dark suspense" — that is, a tale of terror (and sometimes detection) which is realistic in subject matter and treatment, and devoid of supernatural elements.

The trend became particularly apparent when the Horror Writers of America gave their Bram Stoker Award for Best Novel to Thomas Harris's *The Silence of the Lambs* last year. The previous year, Peter Straub's non-fantastic *Koko* won

the World *Fantasy* Award. We also note that David Schow's first novel, aggressively marketed as horror, was the realistic crime-thriller *The Kill Riff.* At that particular World Fantasy Convention in Nashville, Schow jokingly observed that there seemed to be more free advance reading copies of the book than there were attendees.

That many of these books in question are excellent works of fiction, as gripping and suspenseful as you could ever want, is beside the point. Many of our leading writers seem to have grown bored with supernaturalism or merely wish to avoid stagnation by trying something new; that is their business — and perfectly valid as long as they have an audience.

Fine. But we see the horror field losing definition. If this goes on, it will quietly merge into crime fiction and vanish.

One of the great pioneers of this type of "dark suspense" was none other than *Weird Tales's* own Robert Bloch, whose explorations of the interior of the criminal mind, *The Scarf, The Dead Beat, The Will To Kill, Firebug,* and, most famous of all, *Psycho,* firmly established the form in which Straub, Harris, and Schow, among many others, now excel.

But maybe there is something to be said for genre labels after all. These books were all published as crime fiction. No one would have expected to see such stories in *Weird Tales*® back in the 1940s and '50s, when Bloch was also writing such *fantastic* horror classics as "Yours Truly, Jack the Ripper," "Lucy Comes to Stay," and "The Weird Tailor."

Weird Tales® remains devoted to more-than-mundane horror, tales which are genuinely terrifying, yes, but ones which take us imaginatively into regions we can reach by no other means — certainly not by reading a police report. There are, we think, greater terrors for the mind and soul than a maniac with a knife.

The Dust Jacket

Science Fiction, Fantasy, Horror, Mystery and Illustrated Books... Fantasy Art Originals, Prints, Portfolios and Books

(We also carry video and audio tapes)

Artwork by and courtesy of Stephen E. Fabian

Jack R. Carollo
Bookseller
*Collector and fan
for 37 years*

Send $1.00 for list
(credited with first order)

The Dust Jacket
9835 Robin Road
Niles, Illinois 60648

(708) 965-0114

We also purchase
Books, Art and Collections

If this is a trend, we're going to buck it. For once, let *Weird Tales®* be retrogressive if need be. Already we're probably doing more than any other publisher to keep alive the full range of the otherwise endangered imaginary-scene fantasy — the kind of story written by Robert E. Howard, Clark Ashton Smith, and Lord Dunsany. In horror, we remain devoted to fantasy, to the terror of the *impossible* intrusion into what our characters (and readers) perceive to be reality.

We do not deny the high quality of some of the crime fiction being published nowadays, nor would we suggest that such stories don't have their genuine virtues — nor would we even claim that we don't occasionally enjoy a *Red Dragon* or *Psycho* — but that's not what "weird" fiction is about or what *Weird Tales®* intends to publish. And we think our readers will support us on this.

And now, some enthusiasm from **Christopher Dunn** of Potsdam, NY:

Congratulations on the Bloch Issue (number 300). For me, the best reading was the memoir, "One More Tale to Tell," for its picture of HPL as correspondent-mentor. But, then, I've been an HPL fan since the early 1950s, when I came across "The Rats in the Walls" and "The Dunwich Horror," and have read what I could about him ever since.

Stories: As always, all of them were good — but was it really fair to match the newer authors against a master? To say nothing of springing one-half of Henry Kuttner on them? (There's a Blochian picture.)

To answer, I guess, my own question, I thought "Tap Dancing" and "Rumors of Greatness" were best, in that order, this time (even liked "Mothrasaurus"). "Wager of Dreams" was good enough, too, but I thought the style was reaching a bit far sometimes. But I was struck by the battle-cry, "For the Nonce!" Always been mine too.

And it was not as if they were matched against Bloch alone; Bloch plus Gahan Wilson: an almost unbeatable combination, that seemed to me as perfect as Dunsany and Sime! (God! What a cover picture.)

Robert A.W. Lowndes, the distinguished author, editor, and survivor of the pulp era, comments further on issue 300:

Whenever a new issue of Weird Tales® comes in, I put aside other reading matter and go through all the departments and other non-fiction with much pleasure. (Fiction gets put aside for later on, and I'm always a couple issues behind; but I do read it all.)

There are a couple of items in Robert Bloch's splendid "One More Story to Tell" that call for comment. First, on page 62, is clearly a misprint: Bloch could not have started reading WT in 1937 (and later the correct date is given). That first issue was, of course, the August 1927 one, which went on sale the first of July. While there was nothing by Lovecraft in it, there was a Lovecraft-like story by Frank Belknap Long: "The Man With A Thousand Legs." And all in all, it was a very good issue to start with. (I myself started with the October 1931 issue, and received my introduction to HPL there — one of his best short stories, "The Strange High House in the Mist.")

However, on page 70 we find an outright error by the Grand Master himself. He tells us that the January 1935 issue of WT, which contained his story "The Feast in the Abbey," went on sale November 1st, 1934. No way! Let us go back to the year 1933 for a moment. On March 1, 1933 we saw the April WT (the last one to carry the logo that had been used for the covers since the January 1929 issue), starting a new serial, "Golden Blood," by Jack Williamson. But no new issue appeared on April First. The May number came out April 15th, without any explanation. No new issue appeared in the month of May, but on June 1, we saw the June issue; and in "The Eyrie," editor Wright explains that they had decided to stop pre-dating the magazine, so let the April issue and the May issue stay on sale for a month and a half. Henceforth WT *would be dated according to the calendar month. And so it was until August 1936, when on the first of August we saw the August-September issue. That time we had an explanation, lest anyone fear that the magazine had become a bi-monthly. They had decided that pre-dating by one month was a better thing after all.*

So, you see, that the January 1935 WT *had* to *go on sale January 1st, 1935. Bloch may well have received an advance copy of the issue, but that would have had to be in December 1934, certainly not November.*

Now for a few comments on Weird Tales *in general. (My enclosed renewal check bespeaks my general approval.) The fiction is well-written, but there are some stories which do not strike me as in any way weird; bizarre, yes; unpleasant, yes; but that does not constitute weirdness to my eyes. The most recent example I can give you is "The Shaft," by David J. Schow — and now you know how far behind I am in the stories. It's not that it was just another tiresome story about a dope-dealer who gets his; that would have been forgivable to me had I found anything truly weird in the tale. Since I did not, I felt cheated.*

And I cannot express any enthusiasm for your general policy of having each issue entirely illustrated by the same artist. Too often, I have not been attracted or stimulated into reading a story by its illustration — and in at least one issue I didn't care for a single illustration. I realize that there is a certain production advantage in your policy, and, of course, if most readers like the work of the particular artist, you have a winner. (But I can only call 'em as I see 'em.)

The purpose of having one artist illustrate an issue is more than easy production. It's an excuse to showcase a featured artist the way we do featured writers. And there is a crassly practical side to it: artists like to be showcased, and for such an opportunity many artists will go to extraordinary lengths, displaying much greater range than they normally do in a single illustration.

Often, too, the implied honor enables us to get famous artists we might not otherwise be able to afford, *and* it adds a famous signature to the limited edition of the magazine, thus increasing sales of the hardcovers.

At the same time, when we found ourselves forced to do a many-artist issue (e.g., number 298), we found the logistics not to be all that formidable, and the result was so appreciated by the readers that we intend to repeat the experiment with issue 303.

James T. Hughes III has a peculiar complaint:

British writers speak English — not American. As I read their stories, certain foreign colloquialisms get caught in my throat. They go down like raw oysters, and give my mental voice a nasty Cockney accent. It's distracting. It's irritating.

In the Fall 1990 issue there were two stories that were obviously British: "In Her Shoes" and "1/72nd Scale." Both would have been better if somebody had pointed out to the authors words that don't mean anything here in the USA.

There is a style difference between us Yanks and them Limeys as well. It is reminiscent of unforgivable droners like George Eliot — length, pointless (if marginally poetic) descriptions and extensive, unexploited character development — probably a symptom of the kinds of writing taught in school, but who knows?

I don't want no trouble — just had to go on record as saying, "If you exchange with the Brits, translate the foreign

words and 86 the bullshit, because it bugs me." End of snivel.

Don't want no trouble, eh wot, mate? Two of your points are valid: that the British *don't* talk the President's American too good, and that the British style tends to be a bit more leisurely. The very spare Ernest-Hemingway–Dashiel-Hammett–James-T.-Farrell mode seems to be uniquely American. But let's not be too provincial. We can hardly ask the British writers to write in American idiom. The results would be as grotesque as a British actor trying to talk like a Texan. Remember the cowboy character in the Louis Jordan *Dracula*? Like that. It's what a Hollywood English butler must sound like to British ears.

And we can hardly ban British writers from our pages, particularly when so many Britons are popular or even bestsellers in the United States. We think of J.R.R. Tolkien, Ramsey Campbell, Arthur C. Clarke, Tanith Lee, Michael Moorcock, James Herbert, etc. So the "translation" problem can hardly be as severe as you think, at least for most readers.

Besides, with all the British television we get over here, everything from *The Avengers* to *Masterpiece Theatre*, we think most American readers can adjust to an idiom that includes lorries, lifts, roundabouts, car boots and car bonnets, petrol, addresses *in* Charing Cross Road rather than on it, and so on. Not that we recommend that American writers try to write the Queen's English. Many of those television shows are set in the past, and the language we may pick up from them may be decades (sometimes centuries) out of date.

Last time one of us (Darrell) was in London, he was indeed called "guv'nor" by a beggar, but never once did he hear anyone exclaim, "Blimey!"

Frequent correspondent **Greg Koster** takes issue with John Betancourt:

I suppose that Mr. Betancourt will be picking out numerous quills, after admitting that he has joined up with a book packager (issue 298). Nevetheless, let me add a few shafts of my own.

1) In his first point, Mr. B lists some of the books that packagers have put out, in an attempt to show that they are "real" books. Conspicuously missing are books by new writers. He has not addressed the critical point of developing new talent. To be sure, shared-universe books (such as Robot City*) are written by relatively new authors, but who knows who they are? I am unable to remember one author in any of the series, just the fellow who supplied the idea/background.*

Beyond the original sale, what money, let alone recognition, does this supply the writer of these books? Even a "failed" book that comes out under the author's own aegis has a chance of selling later on, after the author's later books have established him. An example of this is C.P. Snow, who wrote seven novels before The Masters *struck it rich for him. Immediately his earlier books began selling much better. Can the authors of* Robot City *et al. have the same confidence? I doubt it.*

2) The assertion that publishers are in the business of making money is far more complicated than it seems. For every author who hits it big the first time out (James Jones, say), there are a lot more who need time to develop. A good example is John Irving, who was published by Random House. His sales were sluggish, and after five novels, Random House said, "Look, kid, we can't publish this book; it's too weird."

So he took The World According to Garp *to Dutton. But it is only hindsight that enables us to laugh at Random House. How many packagers are willing to spend the time (and money) to let an author establish himself, while being fully aware that many of their bets will bust? These uncertainties seem to daunt the packagers, who are trying to cut risk with such strategems as the famous author lending his name and a background.*

3) Mr. B really left himself open on this charge. What's an author to do who is limited to one novel a year and has done his latest in six months? The obvious answer is to turn to the next one, because inevitably there will come a day when a novel will not let itself be finished in a year, let alone six months. I am also appalled at the shot Mr. B takes at short fiction: "Write short stories (which have no guarantee of selling?)" Well, yes. What are we readers who like short stories to do if Mr. B's advice is followed?

I think that Mr. B needs a bit more faith in what packagers do. It seems to me that packagers are primarily concentrating on works of entertainment. This is a respectable, praiseworthy endeavor, despite the efforts of, say, Norman Spinrad to make it taboo.

At the same time, Mr. B seems to be arguing that not only are packagers great entertainers, they are great artists as well. It isn't so. The quantity of high art that has come out of packagers is much too small for the volume of material they put out.

Why not come out openly for entertainment, making no strained assertions that this is also Litrachoor? Surely there is room for both.

Author **Lois Tilton** comments:

In response to your comments in issue 299 on the subject of the small press: I noticed that I wasn't listed as one of the new writers published by WT, *but if not an absolute novice I'm certainly not a famous name; yet my story "The Highwayman" in 292 was only my third professional sale, and I consider* Weird Tales® *quite open to newer writers.*

It's the small press that I've always found inaccessible. I can count close to a dozen story sales by this time, mostly to pro markets. But whenever I submit to the small press, my usual response is a form rejection, most often after a wait of too many months. But those were all trunk stories, right? No, not at all. The fact of the matter is, in the horror field there are far too few magazine markets for short fiction. The small press fills a real need, and I'd really like to support their efforts, even if it isn't going to make me rich or famous. But they make it awfully damn hard to try.

I've sometimes speculated that my failure with small-press editors is because I'm not a known name — in the small-press field, where the same writers seem to appear with a decided regularity. In my experience, at any rate, it's the small press that seems to be a closed shop, not the pro markets.

The reason we didn't list you as one of our "discoveries" is, indeed, that we buy *stories* instead of authors' names, so we didn't check up on your background first. The same happened when we thought we had "discovered" Robert Sampson, only to find out later that he'd been published as far back as 1954. We agree that the small press is valuable, but we think that authors should go into it with both eyes open, with the perspective that this small-town theater isn't Broadway.

But when the small press closes itself off into a *field* unto itself, that's unhealthy. There shouldn't be such a thing as a "small-press writer," as opposed to a writer who publishes in the small press. Of our present staff, Darrell publishes in the small press regularly (mostly *Weirdbook* and *Marion Zimmer Bradley's Fantasy Magazine* these days, but extensively over the years); but he by no means considers himself a small-press writer.

The Most Popular Story in issue 299 is hard to determine. We *need* your votes to make this poll meaningful. There weren't enough votes this time to let us say more than that "Stalin's Teardrops" by Ian Watson seems to be out in front. So, please, let us hear from you. Ω

THE DEN

by John Gregory Betancourt

As you buy books in the spring and summer, think about this: they are far more likely to be award nominees than books published later in the year. Why? Because of the lag time in the award nomination process.

For example, if you are an active member of the Science Fiction Writers of America, you are entitled to nominate and vote for the Nebula Awards, which cover works published in the previous year. If you are nominating works for the 1990 Nebula Awards, your list of nominees must be received by January, 1991 — which doesn't give the November and December books much time to get out there and get read.

Which isn't to say there aren't ways around the system. Advance reading copies are often available. And, in the case of the Nebula Awards, any edition can be withdrawn in favor of a later one (useful primarily when the first edition is a small-print-run hardcover). This rule for withdrawing an edition can be stretched a bit, though, which is one reason the Nebula Awards process is currently being revamped . . . Roger MacBride Allen just withdrew the paperback edition of *The Ring of Charon* (TOR, December 1990) in favor of the Science Fiction Book Club edition (January 1991) for obvious reasons!

To the reviews:

Maps in a Mirror: The Short Fiction of Orson Scott Card,
by Orson Scott Card.
TOR Books, hardcover, 675 pp., $22.95

When I first saw the title, I thought this book was non-fiction dealing with Card's short work. It's not. It's a collection of nearly all of Card's short fiction to date, encompassing 46 stories and nearly 40,000 words of new material (mostly essays and memoirs about the writing of the material here). It also includes a goodly number of stories which Card says he won't allow to be reprinted again. Several have been expanded into novels: "Mikal's Songbird" was expanded into *Songmaster* and "Ender's Game" was expanded into his novel of the same title. It also includes several children's stories originally written for Mormon periodicals (Card is very active in the Mormon community).

The Cipher,
by Kathe Koja.
Dell, 356 pp., $4.50

Many critics are hailing *The Cipher* as a new classic, but for the life of me I don't understand why. I think it may be a case of too much hype for a new writer and a new publishing program, with everyone too eager to jump on the bandwagon before they miss Something Special.

The story is pretty straightforward: Nicholas has found a black-hole-like object in a storage room in his apartment building. When he tells his sometimes-girlfriend Nakota, she takes a perverse interest in it, and allows their romance to rekindle. She is using Nicholas to conduct private experiments — usually dropping small animals into the hole to see what happens to them (they mutate weirdly). Things get out of control when the hole begins taking over her mind, and when Nicholas stops her, he ends up with his hand down the hole.

Suddenly he has a hole *in* his hand, and it's oozing . . . *stuff.*

The problems with the book stem not from its plot (which is interesting and novel), but from unsympathetic characters and murky, hard-to-wade-through prose. The writing is simply not very good stream-of-consciousness, as when they go to visit the hole:

. . . From the first she was first, me hanging a little behind, her idea to wield the flashlight (no good), her idea to throw something down it (an asphalt rock plucked from the parking lot, not too big and not too small; it made no sound, no sound at all, can you imagine how spooky that is?). An empty glass: nothing, though the glass was warm when it came back, the heavy string that held it warm too. A camera, my single idea, but we never did, couldn't figure out how to make it work, and we couldn't afford one that would shoot by itself. A piece of paper,

The
New York Review
of Science Fiction

Art by Daniel M. Pinkwater

Criticism, Reviews, and the Unexpected

her idea (that should have been mine, some poet I am) but nothing still.

Talking it over, and over and over, theories abundant, her eyes slitted and hands not so much expressive as martial, me with my hesitancy and my beer, building fences for her to jump.

The Cipher is the debut book in Dell's new Abyss horror line, which promises some interesting books in the coming months. Perhaps my expectations were too high, based on all the hype. Or perhaps I'm merely too dense to pick up on its brilliance. Whatever the case, *The Cipher* is one I'd just as soon have missed.

Short Story Paperbacks.
Pulphouse Publishing, $1.95 (each)

You have to give the Pulphouse people credit: they are always at the forefront of small-press innovation. Their latest idea is Short Story Paperbacks, which are exactly what they sound like: each is a single short story published in paperback format, with two-color covers. They plan to release ten (!) Short Story Paperbacks every other month. The first ten were released in January:

1: "Loser's Night," by Poul Anderson
2: "A Case of Painter's Ear," by John Brunner
3: "Xolotl," by Robert Sheckley
4: "All the Clocks are Melting," by Bruce Boston
5: "Blossoms," by Kim Antieau
6: "Ecce Hominid," by Esther Friesner
7: "A Case of Mistaken Identity," by L. Timmel Duchamp
8: "The Cutter," by Ed Bryant
9: "Yours Truly, Jack the Ripper," by Robert Bloch
10: "The Girl Who Fell Into the Sky," by Kate Wilhelm.

Five are originals and five are reprints; in the future, all titles will be reprints (which I feel is a mistake: reprints tend to be readily accessible, often — if they're classics like "Yours Truly, Jack the Ripper" — not only in their original appearances, but also in collections, best of the year anthologies, etc.).

The average Short Story Paperback seems to run about 40 pages, which makes for mighty slender volumes. And it costs roughly half the price of the average "real" paperback, so I'm not sure it's the greatest deal in the world.

But do I think they'd sell? Yes. Not because they're a bargain, or because they're great fiction, or because of the line-up of authors. They'll sell, at first, because they're new and different: novelty value. (You have to admit it *is* a neat idea). And they'll keep selling because they're numbered. Once you start collecting a series, it's hard to stop.

They're also accepting subscriptions to the series, which makes the books a bit more affordable: the next 30 books for $55.00, or the next 60 (one year) for $100.00.

Order from: Pulphouse Publishing, PO Box 1227, Eugene OR 97440.

The Silence of the Lambs,
by Thomas Harris.
St. Martin's Press, 367 pp., $5.95

Serial killers are big these days. They have slashed their way through horror million-copy-plus best-seller lists with titles such as Rex Miller's *Slob* (and its sequels); they have titillated the masses in non-fiction and "fictionalizations" of actual serial-murder cases.

One of those making the biggest — um — *killing* in the fictional chronicles of mass-murder is Thomas Harris. *The Silence of the Lambs* is a quasi-sequel to his previous best-seller, *Red Dragon*. Yes, it's an old book (1988); but the movie based on it has just been released, and St. Martin's Press is pushing it hard once again. It already has two million copies in print, and I expect it will sell another million or so before everything lets up.

It *is* a good book. Clarice Starling, a young trainee who wants to be an FBI agent more than anything else, gets recruited for a special project involving a new mass-murderer the papers are calling Buffalo Bill. The only person who may be able to help the FBI crack the case is another mass-murderer, the brilliant (and currently incarcerated) psychologist and serial killer, Dr. Hannibal ("the cannibal") Lector. And Lector seems willing to help, but he only wants to talk to Clarice. It seems he has his own private agenda. . . .

There is no supernatural element in *The Silence of the Lambs,* but that doesn't make the horrors any less horrible. Because the characters are so real, because the attention to detail is so great, because *this could happen,* Harris grabs the reader by the throat and doesn't let go. It's an intense, dark novel. Recommended.

In short:

Journal Wired is a weird little book that sure looks like a magazine, even though everyone associated with it insists it's not. The most recent issue I've seen is dated Summer/Fall 1990 and is, alas, the last. It's a large trade paperback, 353 pages in length, with oddball and esoteric contributions by a number of science-fiction, fantasy, horror, rock-&-roll, and unclassifiable people: Allen Steele, Jonathan Lethem, Lucius Shepard, Robert Frazier, Patrick McGrath, Wayne Allen Sallee, and more. Lots of fiction and non-fiction, a few interviews, letters. $15.00 from: Mark V. Ziesing, PO Box 76, Shingletown CA 96088.

Grue #12 has appeared. In many ways, *Grue* is my favorite of all the small-press horror magazines. It has a definite style and personality, an attractive format, generally good fiction, and it appears on schedule (thrice yearly). The current issue contains 11 stories and 11 poems. Authors include Wayne Allen Sallee and Nina Kiriki Hoffman. $4.50 (3/$13.00) from: Hell's Kitchen Productions, PO Box 370, Times Square Station, New York NY 10108-0370. The back cover now bears a "Warning! Contains Adult Material" label. Take note, if you're squeamish about such things. Ω

THE SAME IN ANY LANGUAGE

by Ramsey Campbell

Walters / after Böcklin

The day my father is to take me where the lepers used to live is hotter than ever. Even the old women with black scarves wrapped around their heads sit inside the bus station instead of on the chairs outside the tavernas. Kate fans herself with her straw hat like a basket someone's sat on and gives my father one of those smiles they've made up between them. She's leaning forwards to see if that's our bus when he says, "Why do you think they call them lepers, Hugh?"

I can hear what he's going to say, but I have to humour him. "I don't know."

"Because they never stop leaping up and down."

It takes him much longer to say the first four words than the rest of it. I groan because he expects me to, and Kate lets off one of her giggles I keep hearing whenever they stay in my father's and my room at the hotel and send me down for a swim. "If you can't give a grin, give a groan," my father says for about the millionth time, and Kate pokes him with her freckly elbow as if he's too funny for words. She annoys me so much that I say, "Lepers don't rhyme with creepers, Dad."

"I never thought they did, son. I was just having a laugh. If we can't laugh we might as well be dead, ain't that straight, Kate?" He winks at her thigh and slaps his own instead, and says to me, "Since you're so clever, why don't you find out when our bus is coming?"

"That's it now."

"And I'm Hercules." He lifts up his fists to make his muscles bulge for Kate and says, "You're telling us that tripe spells A Flounder?"

"Elounda, Dad. It does. The letter like a **Y** upside-down is how they write an **L**."

"About time they learned how to write properly, then," he says, staring around to show he doesn't care who hears. "Well, there it is if you really want to trudge around another old ruin instead of having a swim."

"I expect he'll be able to do both once we get to the village," Kate says, but I can tell she's hoping I'll just swim. "Will you two gentlemen see me across the road?"

My mother used to link arms with me and my father when he was living with us. "I'd better make sure it's the right bus," I say, and run out so fast I can pretend I didn't hear my father calling me back.

A man with skin like a boot is walking backwards in the dust behind the bus, shouting "Elounda" and waving his arms as if he's pulling the bus into the space in line. I sit on a seat opposite two Germans who block the aisle until they've taken off their rucksacks, but my father finds three seats together at the rear. "Aren't you with us, Hugh?" he shouts, and everyone on the bus looks at him.

When I see him getting ready to shout again I walk down the aisle. I'm hoping nobody notices me, but Kate says loudly, "It's a pity you ran off like that, Hugh. I was going to ask if you'd like an ice cream."

"No thank you," I say, trying to sound like my mother when she was only just speaking to my father, and step over Kate's legs. As the bus rumbles uphill I turn as much of my back on her as I can, and watch the streets.

Agios Nikolaos looks as if they haven't finished building it. Some of the tavernas are on the bottom floors of blocks with no roofs, and sometimes there are more tables on the pavements outside than in. The bus goes downhill again as if it's hiccuping, and when it reaches the bottomless lake where young people with no children stay in the hotels with discos, it follows the edge of the bay. I watch the white boats on the blue water, but really I'm seeing the conductor coming down the aisle and feeling as if a lump's growing in my stomach from me wondering what my father will say to him.

The bus is climbing beside the sea when he reaches us. "Three for leper land," my father says.

The conductor stares at him and shrugs. "As far as you go," Kate says, and rubs herself against my father. "All the way."

When the conductor pushes his lips forwards out of his moustache and beard my father begins to get angry, unless he's pretending. "Where you kept your lepers. Spiny Lobster or whatever you call the damned place."

"It's Spinalonga, Dad, and it's off the coast from where we're going."

"I know that, and he should." My father is really angry now. "Did you get that?" he says to the conductor. "My ten-year-old can speak your lingo, so don't tell me you can't speak ours."

The conductor looks at me, and I'm afraid he wants me to talk Greek. My mother gave me a little computer that translates words into Greek when you type them, but I've left it at the hotel because my father said it sounded like a bird which only knew one note. "We're going to Elounda, please," I stammer.

"Elounda, boss," the conductor says to me. He takes the money from my father without looking at him and gives me the tickets and change. "Fish is good by the harbour in the evening," he says, and goes to sit next to the driver while the bus swings round the zigzags of the hill road.

My father laughs for the whole bus to hear. "They think you're so important, Hugh, you won't be wanting to go home to your mother."

Kate strokes his head as if he's her pet, then she turns to me. "What do you like most about Greece?"

She's trying to make friends with me like when she kept saying I should call her Kate, only now I see it's for my father's sake. All she's done is make me think how the magic places seemed to have lost their magic because my mother wasn't there with me, even Knossos where Theseus killed the Minotaur. There were just a few corridors left that might have been the maze he was supposed to find his way out of, and my father let me stay in them for a while, but then he lost his temper because all the guided tours were in foreign languages and nobody could tell him how to get back to the coach. We nearly got stuck overnight in Heraklion, when he'd promised to take Kate for dinner that night by the bottomless pool in Agios Nikolaos. "I don't know," I mumble, and gaze out the window.

"I like the sun, don't you? And the people when they're being nice, and the lovely, clear sea."

It sounds to me as if she's getting ready to send me off swimming again. They met while I was, our second morning at the hotel. When I came out of the sea my father had moved his towel next to hers and she was giggling. I watch Spinalonga Island float over the horizon like a ship made of rock and grey towers, and hope she'll think I'm agreeing with her if that means she'll leave me alone. But she says, "I suppose most boys are morbid at your age. Let's hope you'll grow up to be like your father."

She's making it sound as if the leper colony is the only place I've wanted to visit, but it's just another old place I can tell my mother I've been. Kate doesn't want to go there because she doesn't like old places — she said if Knossos was a palace she was glad she's not a queen. I don't speak to her again until the bus has stopped by the harbour.

There aren't many tourists, even in the shops and tavernas lined up along the winding pavement. Greek people who look as if they were born in the sun sit drinking at tables under awnings like stalls in a market. Some priests who I think at first are wearing black hat boxes on their heads march by, and fishermen come up from their boats with octopuses on sticks like big kebabs.

The bus turns round in a cloud of dust and petrol fumes while Kate hangs onto my father with one hand and flaps the front of her flowery dress with the other. A boatman stares at the tops of her boobs which make me think of spotted fish and shouts "Spinalonga" with both hands round his mouth.

"We've hours yet," Kate says. "Let's have a drink. Hugh may even get that ice cream if he's good."

If she's going to talk about me as though I'm not there I'll do my best not to be. She and my father sit under an awning and I kick dust on the pavement outside until she says, "Come under, Hugh. We don't want you with sunstroke."

I don't want her pretending she's my mother, but if I say so I'll only spoil the day more than she already has. I shuffle to the table next to the one she's sharing with my father and throw myself on a chair. "Well, Hugh," she says, "do you want one?"

"No thank you," I say, even though the thought of an ice cream or a drink starts my mouth trying to drool.

"You can have some of my lager if it ever arrives," my father says at the top of his voice, and stares hard at some Greeks sitting at a table. "Anyone here a waiter?" he says, lifting his hand to his mouth as if he's holding a glass.

When all the people at the table smile and raise their glasses and shout cheerily at him, Kate says, "I'll find someone and then I'm going to the little girls' room while you men have a talk."

My father watches her crossing the road and gazes at the doorway of the taverna once she's gone in. He's quiet for a while, then he says, "Are you going to be able to say you had a good time?"

I know he wants me to enjoy myself when I'm with him, but I also think what my mother stopped herself from saying to me is true — that he booked the holiday in Greece as a way of scoring off her by taking me somewhere she'd always wanted to go. He stares at the taverna as if he can't move until I let him, and I say, "I expect so, if we go to the island."

"That's my boy. Never give in too easily." He smiles at me with one side of his face. "You don't mind if I have some fun as well, do you?"

He's making it sound as if he wouldn't have had much fun if it had just been the two of us, and I think that was how he'd started to feel before he met Kate. "It's your holiday," I say.

He's opening his mouth after another long silence when Kate comes out of the taverna with a man carrying two lagers and a lemonada on a tray. "See that you thank her," my father tells me.

I didn't ask for lemonada. He said I could have some lager. I say, "Thank you very much" and feel my throat tightening as I gulp the lemonada, because her eyes are saying she's won.

"That must have been welcome," she says when I put down the empty glass. "Another? Then I should find yourself something to do. Your father and I may be here for a while."

"Have a swim," my father suggests.

"I haven't brought my cossy."

"Neither have those boys," Kate says, pointing at the harbour. "Don't worry, I've seen boys wearing less."

My father smirks behind his hand, and I can't bear it. I run to the jetty the boys are diving off, and drop my T-shirt and shorts on it and my sandals on top of them, and dive in.

The water's cold, but not for long. It's full of little fish that nibble you if you only float, and it's clearer than tap water, so you can see down to the pebbles and the fish pretending to be them. I chase fish and swim underwater and almost catch an octopus before it squirms out to sea. Then three Greek boys about my age swim over, and we're pointing at ourselves and saying our names when I see Kate and my father kissing.

I know their tongues are in each other's mouths — getting some tongue, the kids at my school call it. I feel like swimming away as far as I can go and never coming back. But Stavros and Stathis and Costas are using their hands to tell me we should see who can swim fastest, so I do that instead. Soon I've forgotten my father and Kate, even when we sit on the jetty for a rest before we have more races. It must be hours later when I realise Kate is calling, "Come here a minute."

The sun isn't so hot now. It's reaching under the awning, but she and my father haven't moved back into the shadow. A boatman shouts "Spinalonga" and points at how low the sun is. I don't mind swimming with my new friends instead of going to the island, and I'm about to tell my father so when Kate says, "I've been telling your dad he should be proud of you. Come and see what I've got for you."

They've both had a lot to drink. She almost falls across the table as I go to her. Just as I get there I see what she's going to give me, but it's too late. She grabs my head with both hands and sticks a kiss on my mouth.

She tastes of old lager. Her mouth is wet and bigger than mine, and when it squirms it makes me think of an octopus. "Mmm*mwa,*" it says, and then I manage to duck out of her hands, leaving her blinking at me as if her eyes won't quite work. "Nothing wrong with a bit of loving," she says. "You'll find that out when you grow up."

My father knows I don't like to be kissed, but he's frowning at me as if I should have let her. Suddenly I want to get my own back on them in the only way I can think of. "We need to go to the island now."

"Better go to the loo first," my father says. "They wouldn't have one on the island when all their willies had dropped off."

Kate hoots at that while I'm getting dressed, and I feel as if she's laughing at the way my ribs show through my skin however much I eat. I stop myself from shivering in case she or my father makes out that's a reason for us to go back to the hotel. I'm heading for the toilet when my father says, "Watch out you don't catch anything in there or we'll have to leave you on the island."

I know there are all sorts of reasons why my parents split up, but just now this is the only one I can think of — my mother not being able to stand his jokes and how the more she told him to finish the more he would do it, as if he couldn't stop himself. I run into the toilet, trying not to look at the pedal bin where you have to drop the used paper, and close my eyes once I've taken aim.

Is today going to be what I remember about Greece? My mother brought me up to believe that even the sunlight here had magic in it, and I expected to feel the ghosts of legends in all the old places. If there isn't any magic in the sunlight, I want there to be some in the dark. The thought seems to make the insides of my eyelids darker, and I can smell the drains. I pull the chain and zip myself up, and then I wonder if my father sent me in here so we'll miss the boat. I nearly break the hook on the door, I'm so desperate to be outside.

The boat is still tied to the harbour, but I can't see the boatman. Kate and my father are holding hands across the table, and my father's looking around as though he means to order another drink. I squeeze my eyes shut so hard that when I open them everything's gone black. The blackness fades along with whatever I wished, and I see the boatman kneeling on the jetty, talking to Stavros. "Spinalonga," I shout.

He looks at me, and I'm afraid he'll say it's too late. I feel tears building up behind my eyes. Then he stands up and holds out a hand towards my father and Kate. "One hour," he says.

Kate's gazing after a bus that has just

begun to climb the hill. "We may as well go over as wait for the next bus," my father says, "and then it'll be back to the hotel for dinner."

Kate looks sideways at me. "And after all that he'll be ready for bed," she says like a question she isn't quite admitting to.

"Out like a light, I reckon."

"Fair enough," she says, and uses his arm to get herself up.

The boatman's name is Iannis, and he doesn't speak much English. My father seems to think he's charging too much for the trip until he realises it's that much for all three of us, and then he grins as if he thinks Iannis has cheated himself. "Heave ho then, Janice," he says with a wink at me and Kate.

The boat is about the size of a big rowing-boat. It has a cabin at the front and benches along the sides and a long box in the middle that shakes and smells of petrol. I watch the point of the boat sliding through the water like a knife and feel as if we're on our way to the Greece I've been dreaming of. The white buildings of Elounda shrink until they look like teeth in the mouth of the hills of Crete, and Spinalonga floats up ahead.

It makes me think of an abandoned ship bigger than a liner, a ship so dead that it's standing still in the water without having to be anchored. The evening light seems to shine out of the steep rusty sides and the bony towers and walls high above the sea. I know it was a fort to begin with, but I think it might as well have been built for the lepers. I can imagine them trying to swim to Elounda and drowning because there wasn't enough left of them to swim with, if they didn't just throw themselves off the walls because they couldn't bear what they'd turned into. If I say these things to Kate I bet more than her mouth will squirm — but my father gets in first. "Look, there's the welcoming committee."

Kate gives a shiver that reminds me I'm trying not to feel cold. "Don't say things like that. They're just people like us, probably wishing they hadn't come."

I don't think she can see them any more clearly than I can. Their heads are poking over the wall at the top of the cliff above a little pebbly beach which is the only place a boat can land. There are five or six of them, only I'm not sure they're heads; they might be stones someone has balanced on the wall — they're almost the same colour. I'm wishing I had some binoculars when Kate grabs my father so hard the boat rocks and Iannis waves a finger at her, which doesn't please my father. "You keep your eye on your steering, Janice," he says.

Iannis is already taking the boat toward the beach. He didn't seem to notice the heads on the wall, and when I look again they aren't there. Maybe they belonged to some of the people who are coming down to a boat bigger than Iannis's. That boat chugs away as Iannis's bumps into the jetty. "One hour," he says. "Back here."

He helps Kate onto the jetty while my father glowers at him, then he lifts me out of the boat. As soon as my father steps onto the jetty Iannis pushes the boat out again. "Aren't you staying?" Kate pleads.

He shakes his head and points hard at the beach. "Back here, one hour."

She look as if she wants to run into the water and climb aboard the boat, but my father shoves his arm around her waist. "Don't worry, you've got two fellers to keep you safe, and neither of them with a girl's name."

The only way up to the fort is through a tunnel that bends in the middle so you can't see the end until you're nearly halfway in. I wonder how long it will take for the rest of the island to be as dark as the middle of the tunnel. When Kate sees the end she runs until she's in the open and stares at the sun, which is perched on top of the towers now. "Fancying a climb?" my father says.

She makes a face at him as I walk past her. We're in a kind of street of stone sheds that have mostly caved in. They must be where the lepers lived, but there are only shadows in them now, not even birds. "Don't go too far, Hugh," Kate says.

"I want to go all the way round, otherwise it wasn't worth coming."

"I don't, and I'm sure your father expects you to consider me."

"Now, now, children," my father says. "Hugh can do as he likes as long as he's careful and the same goes for us, eh, Kate?"

I can tell he's surprised when she doesn't laugh. He looks unsure of himself and angry about it, the way he did when he and my mother were getting ready to tell me they were splitting up. I run along the line of huts and think of hiding in one so I can jump out at Kate. Maybe they aren't empty after all; something rattles in one as if bones are crawling about in the dark. It could be a snake under part of the roof that's fallen. I keep running until I come to steps leading up from the street to the top of the island, where most of the light is, and I've started jogging up them when Kate shouts, "Stay where we can see you. We don't want you hurting yourself."

"It's all right, Kate; leave him be," my father says. "He's sensible."

"If I'm not allowed to speak to him, I don't know why you invited me at all."

I can't help grinning as I sprint to the top of the steps and duck out of sight behind a grassy mound that makes me think of a grave. From up here I can see the whole island, and we aren't alone on it. The path I've run up from leads all round the island, past more huts and towers and a few bigger buildings, and then it goes down to the tunnel. Just before it does it passes the wall above the beach, and between the path and the

wall there's a stone yard full of slabs. Some of the slabs have been moved away from holes like long boxes full of soil or darkness. They're by the wall where I thought I saw heads looking over at us. They aren't there now, but I can see heads bobbing down towards the tunnel. Before long they'll be behind Kate and my father.

Iannis is well on his way back to Elounda. His boat is passing one that's heading for the island. Soon the sun will touch the hills. If I went down to the huts I'd see it sink with me and drown. Instead I lie on the mound and look over the island, and see more of the boxy holes hiding behind some of the huts. If I went closer I could see how deep they are, but I quite like not knowing — if I was Greek I expect I'd think they lead to the underworld where all the dead live. Besides, I like being able to look down on my father and Kate and see them trying to see me.

I stay there until Iannis's boat is back at Elounda and the other one has almost reached Spinalonga, and the sun looks as if it's gone down to the hills for a rest. Kate and my father are having an argument. I expect it's about me, though I can't hear what they're saying; the darker it gets between the huts the more Kate waves her arms. I'm getting ready to let my father see me when she screams.

She's jumped back from a hut which has a hole behind it. "Come out, Hugh. I know it's you," she cries.

I can tell what my father's going to say, and I cringe. "Is that you, Hugh? Yoo-hoo," he shouts.

I won't show myself for a joke like that. He leans into the hut through the spiky stone window, then he turns to Kate. "It wasn't Hugh. There's nobody."

I can only just hear him, but I don't have to strain to hear Kate. "Don't tell me that," she cries. "You're both too fond of jokes."

She screams again, because someone's

come running up the tunnel. "Everything all right?" this man shouts. "There's a boat about to leave if you've had enough."

"I don't know what you two are doing," Kate says like a duchess to my father, "but I'm going with this gentleman."

My father calls to me twice. If I go with him I'll be letting Kate win. "I don't think our man will wait," the new one says.

"It doesn't matter," my father says, so fiercely that I know it does. "We've our own boat coming."

"If there's a bus before you get back I won't be hanging around," Kate warns him.

"Please yourself," my father says, so loud that his voice goes into the tunnel. He stares after her as she marches away; he must be hoping she'll change her mind. But I see her step off the jetty into the boat, and it moves out to sea as if the ripples are pushing it to Elounda.

My father puts a hand to his ear as the sound of the engine fades. "So every bugger's left me now, have they?" he says in a kind of shout at himself. "Well, good riddance."

He's waving his fists as if he wants to punch something, and he sounds as if he's suddenly got drunk. He must have been holding it back when Kate was there. I've never seen him like this. It frightens me, so I stay where I am.

It isn't only my father that frightens me. There's only a little bump of the sun left above the hills of Crete now, and I'm afraid how dark the island may be once that goes. Bits of sunlight shiver on the water all the way to the island, and I think I see some heads above the wall of the yard full of slabs, against the light. Which side of the wall are they on? The light's too dazzling; it seems to pinch the sides of the heads so they look thinner than any heads I've ever seen. Then I notice a boat setting out from Elounda, and I squint at it until I'm sure it's Iannis's boat.

He's coming early to fetch us. Even that frightens me, because I wonder why he is. Doesn't he want us to be on the island now he realizes how dark it's getting? I look at the wall, and the heads have gone. Then the hills put the sun out, and it feels as if the island is buried in darkness.

I can still see my way down — the steps are paler than the dark — and I don't like being alone now that I've started shivering. I back off from the mound, because I don't like to touch it, and almost back into a shape with bits of its head poking out and arms that look as if they've dropped off at the elbows. It's a cactus. I'm just standing up when my father says, "There you are, Hugh."

He can't see me yet. He must have heard me gasp. I go to the top of the steps, but I can't see him for the dark. Then his voice moves away. "Don't start hiding again. Looks like we've seen the last of Kate; but we've got each other, haven't we?"

He's still drunk. He sounds as if he's talking to somebody nearer to him than I am. "All right, we'll wait on the beach," he says, and his voice echoes. He's gone into the tunnel, and he thinks he's following me. "I'm here, Dad," I shout so loud that I squeak.

"I heard you, Hugh. Wait there. I'm coming." He's walking deeper into the tunnel. While he's in there my voice must seem to be coming from beyond the far end. I'm sucking in a breath that tastes dusty, so I can tell him where I am, when he says, "Who's that?" with a laugh that almost shakes his words to pieces.

He's met whoever he thought was me when he was heading for the tunnel. I'm holding my breath — I can't breathe or swallow — and I don't know if I feel hot or frozen. "Let me past," he says as if he's trying to make his voice as big as the tunnel. "My son's waiting for me on the beach."

There are so many echoes in the tunnel I'm not sure what I'm hearing besides him. I think there's a lot of shuffling; and the other noise must be voices, because my father says, "What kind of language do you call that? You sound drunker than I am. I said my son's waiting."

He's talking even louder as if that'll make him understood. I'm embarrassed, but I'm more afraid for him. "Dad," I nearly scream, and run down the steps as fast as I can without falling.

"See, I told you. That's my son," he says as if he's talking to a crowd of idiots. The shuffling starts moving like a slow march, and he says, "All right, we'll all go to the beach together. What's the matter with your friends, too drunk to walk?"

I reach the bottom of the steps, hurting my ankles, and run along the ruined street because I can't stop myself. The shuffling sounds as if it's growing thinner, as if the people with my father are leaving bits of themselves behind, and the voices are changing too — they're looser. Maybe the mouths are getting bigger somehow. But my father's laughing, so loud that he might be trying to think of a joke. "That's what I call a hug. No harder, love, or I won't have any puff left," he says to someone. "Come on then; give us a kiss. They're the same in any language."

All the voices stop, but the shuffling doesn't. I hear it go out of the tunnel and onto the pebbles, and then my father tries to scream as if he's swallowed something that won't let him. I scream for him and dash into the tunnel, slipping on things that weren't on the floor when we first came through, and fall out onto the beach.

My father's in the sea. He's already so far out that the water is up to his neck. About six people who look stuck together and to him are walking him away as if they don't need to breathe when their heads start to sink. Bits of them

© '91 Walters

27

float away on the waves my father makes as he throws his arms about and gurgles. I try to run after him, but I've got nowhere when his head goes underwater. The sea pushes me back on the beach, and I run crying up and down it until Iannis comes.

It doesn't take him long to find my father once he understands what I'm saying. Iannis wraps me in a blanket and hugs me all the way to Elounda, and the police take me back to the hotel.

Kate gets my mother's number and calls her, saying she's someone at the hotel who's looking after me because my father's drowned; and I don't care what she says, I just feel numb. I don't start screaming until I'm on the plane back to England, because then I dream that my father has come back to tell a joke. "That's what I call getting some tongue," he says, leaning his face close to mine and showing me what's in his mouth.   Ω

GRIFFIN GOLD

In Arimaspia the streets glitter by night
Torchflames multiplied by walls of gold.
Arimaspi shimmer in the sun
With torques, bands for heads and arms and ankles,
Rings and chains and pins,
And artificial eyes
For gold-hunters
Pecked or clawed at by the griffins
They had robbed.
The oracles in all the lands about
Are bright with Arimaspian offerings,
But still the Arimaspian sky
Echoes by night
With cries of angry griffins
Beating through the air
Searching for unprotected gold-hunters
And revenge.
In Arimaspia they sleep poorly,
Their dreams disturbed beneath the coverlets
Of cloth of gold.

"The northern parts of Europe are very much richer in gold than any other region . . . The one-eyed Arimaspi purloin it from the griffins."— Herodotus, III.116.

— **Ruth Berman**

BAIT

by Ramsey Campbell

"That light is all that is left of your life," Lord Robert said, gesturing negligently toward the torch set in its niche in the wall opposite that to which Thomas was chained. "Though perhaps I should not be so niggardly. You would scarcely have time to savour the attentions of your new companion. Perhaps when you have had a taste of the dark, I may return to discover whether your thoughts are of your wife or of what will visit you."

He turned away. Then, as if inspired, he swung back and slit Thomas's forearm with his sword. A minute later Thomas heard the door slam stoutly, amid the new stone which walled off this extremity of the cellars. The torch-flame streamed away from the gust, dragging its niche and part of the wall by their shadows.

Thomas slid down to squat on the damp stone floor. The short chains gyved to his ankles collected in a heap beneath his thighs, cutting dully into them, but he squatted unmoving. The wall before him panted with the flame.

The light reached out along the grey stone and fell back, unable to maintain its grip. At its farthest reach it snatched forward what Thomas had taken to be part of the darkness: a fissure in the grey wall, moist-edged as a wound. From its apex plopped a slow deliberate drip, mud-thick. Within the fissure, muffled and distant, Thomas heard an awakening scrape of claws.

Rats, he told himself. They must be the companions he had been promised. He hoped they would find him dead. He hoped death would come to him softly as sleep, and as quickly. He closed his eyes and let the plump drip pace his breathing, slow his thoughts. But the flame tyrannized his eyelids, demanding that he watch the light plucking nervously at the fissure.

Already the light was fading, unless a clinging shadow of sleep was gathering on his eyes. Deep in the fissure the claws scraped, growing bolder. He stared into the unsteady cleft of darkness and tried to coax its depths to draw him into sleep. The depths only filled with his memories, the hut at the edge of the forest, Marie.

Marie was crying. "Don't let him take me, I couldn't bear it. If he takes me I won't be yours." Thomas's friends were nodding their heads angrily. "He has no right," they said. "Someone must stand against him. We would have if we'd known. It only needs someone to tell him we know there is no such right, and he will never dare claim it again. We'll stand by you."

Marie was screaming, for Lord Robert had thrown open the door of their hut. Behind him at a distance, blurred and surreptitious in the twilight, Thomas's friends peered. Thomas stood before Marie, warding off Lord Robert. "There is no lord's right, no other lord claims it. You cannot have her. The other lords will come to our aid if you try."

Lord Robert did not speak. His sword, infamous for its sharpness that clove men as a scythe mows grass, trembled a fingernail's breadth from Thomas's eye. Through the doorway Thomas saw that his friends had retreated behind their barred doors. Lord Robert gazed at Marie and held his sword carelessly at Thomas's face until Thomas fell back.

Marie was screaming, no longer in terror of her husband's fate but of her own. She was hugging her breasts and pressing her legs together closely as Lord Robert's lips. Lord Robert threatened her with the sword, prodding her gently with it here and there, each time drawing blood. Abruptly he seemed to tire of trying to persuade her. In a moment he had deflowered her expertly with the sword. After a while he silenced her cries with the blade.

Thomas stood drained of all feeling, too drained even to impale himself on the sword. He waited for the blade to cut him down, but Lord Robert was speaking. "Since you desire a companion who will be yours alone, you shall have one."

The turnkey had led Thomas through the cellars, his torchlight glancing at huddles of chain and starved flesh. Behind Thomas, Lord Robert's sword was ready in its scabbard, a fang in a snake's mouth. When the turnkey had unlocked the door in the depths of the cellars, he'd thrust his light through the opening so sharply that the darkness had almost gulped it up. He'd held the light while Lord Robert had fettered Thomas; then, at a gesture from his master, he'd niched the torch and had fled beyond the new stone wall. Now Thomas wondered dully what that wall had been built to contain.

The torch was sputtering. The cellar wall gasped feebly as its light drained. Thomas was trying to determine how close the sounds within the fissure were, the sounds of something hard scratching faintly and stealthily against stone — he was trying to think how rats could make so measured and purposeful a sound — when darkness doused everything.

The chains bruised his thighs, which throbbed. He wished he had moved before. Now, if he moved, he would betray himself to the rats, which would fasten unseen on him. Unseen: that was the worst, as Lord Robert had intended.

It denied Thomas the chance to fend them off before they reached him. It denied him everything save the sounds of encirclement, the tearing of sharp teeth.

He moved, spreading the chains on either side of him. Let the rats come, he would best them yet. Without the nagging of the iron links, he could sleep. Lord Robert was starving his body to weaken him, but had forgotten that he had already starved Thomas's soul. All Thomas need do was let himself sink into the void he had become. Not even rats could awaken him from that sleep.

But sleep hung back, its presence close yet impalpable as the dark. As Thomas tried to muffle himself in sleep, strove to calm himself so that it could take hold of him, part of him remained doggedly alert to the sounds within the fissure. He tried to judge if they were approaching, to satisfy the sleepless part of him, but each time he had almost grasped their distance the slow drip interrupted, distracting him. The hushed claws scraped in the dark. The drip prodded Thomas awake. Exhausted, he forced himself to listen. The drip pulled his mind down, down into sleep.

He awoke in the forest. Lips were moving timidly over his cheek. It was Marie. He opened his eyes gradually. Above him, swarms of leaves drifted gently over one another; pools of light rippled over him, soft as breath. He couldn't see Marie, for she was kissing his forearm shyly. If he raised his head he would see her. He awoke, and a tongue was lapping thirstily at his sword-wound in the dark.

He roared and kicked out, until the fetters wrenched his ankles. Amid his terror was a deeper horror, that his mind had accepted what Lord Robert had given him in exchange for Marie, accepted it even if only in sleep. He thrust the thing from him, and his hand touched an arm. He felt bone and dust-stubbled wiry muscle, that twitched his fingers away, but no flesh at all. Then the thing scuttled dryly back into the fissure.

Thomas held himself still, though the links bit into his thighs. The lethargic drip mocked the scurrying of his heart. Now he knew why the turnkey had fled, knew the extent of Lord Robert's cruelty. Thomas had heard tales of hungry cadavers that roamed from their graves at night, writhed where they lay impaled beneath crossroads, tapped stealthily at doors to be let in. Only Lord Robert could have made a pet of such a thing. Thomas's folded legs trembled, blazing with pain, but he held himself still, clinging to the silence.

When the hollow scrape of bone emerged from the fissure onto the cellar floor he began to roar like a beast in a fire, shaking his chains. There was nothing else he could do. In a moment he froze aghast, for his noise might have allowed the thing to creep to his side unheard.

But it was scuttling back into the cleft. He listened to the aimless shuffling of bone, and thought the darkness was deceiving him until he remembered how the thing had waited for the light to fail. Suddenly he realized why it had delayed until he had fallen asleep. It was as timid as anything else that might crawl from a hole in a rock.

It was less timid now that it had tasted its victim. The tentative dry groping retreated into the cleft when Thomas shouted and rang his chains against the stone, but each time it came closer to him. Soon it failed to retreat even as far as the wall. He roared and shook the chains desperately, but his noises seemed to be snatched away at once and muffled, scarcely echoing. They hardly stirred the air, which hung damply upon him, dragging him down into sleep.

He sawed his wrists against the gyves to fend off sleep. Then he clutched his wrists, gasping. He had almost drawn blood and offered it for feasting. When he touched the sword-wound and found it moist, he plastered it with gritty mud from the floor. He hammered his elbows against the wall to keep himself awake. Nearby in the blindness he heard bone scrabbling toward him over the floor.

The dark nestled against him, urging the bony claws forward. It settled insidiously about his mind and held him more tightly than the gyves, imprisoned him outside time, choked off his furious sounds. It pressed faces of bone and working muscle against his eyes, jarring him awake. It flooded his mind entirely, while the thirsty bones crept closer.

Lord Robert returned to Thomas several hours after leaving him. He motioned the turnkey to precede him beyond the partition wall, then he took the nervous torch from the man and gestured him out. Holding the torch above Thomas, he gazed down at the slumped unmoving figure from which iron links spilled.

"You have days yet, perhaps weeks," Lord Robert said. "The last man to wear your chains lived for a month, for the others heard his screams. They found your new companion crouched over him like a spider, and you will know it has a spider's appetite. The wall was meant to help it hoard its attentions for those who most deserved them. I am glad they were kept for you."

Thomas did not move. "You are not dead," Lord Robert said, "nor yet so weak that sleep may shield you from me. Show me your face while I prepare you further."

Still Thomas squatted, huddled into himself. Lord Robert thrust the torch into its niche and stooped to Thomas, grasping his hair. The tip of the scabbard touched the floor.

As the hilt inclined toward him Thomas snatched the sword. His chains betrayed his movement, the hilt rang dully against the wall, but the razor-keen blade pierced Lord Robert's groin.

The point glanced from bone and, slipping upward, emerged beside his spine.

Though Lord Robert screamed and writhed heavily, Thomas held the hilt fast until his captive fainted. Presently the turnkey's scared face peered in. The door slammed at once, and Thomas heard the key turn.

Lord Robert found himself propped against the wall next to Thomas, impaled on the sword. His cloak lay across Thomas's knees. Thomas gazed at him while he moaned. "I shall call the turnkey," Lord Robert said, not daring to move on the sword. "He will free you and escort you unchallenged from my castle and my domain. None shall pursue you."

"The turnkey has imprisoned us both," Thomas said, lifting the blade.

"Stand up. You will be my bait. We shall see if your sword will destroy your pet."

Lord Robert obeyed. He stood before Thomas, moving with minute delicacy on the axis of the sword. Sweat poured down his face. When Thomas withdrew the blade slowly until the point was flush with his captive's back, Lord Robert moaned but stood firm.

"Let him come now," Thomas said. Within the fissure an impatient desiccated rattling had ventured almost to the edge of the light. "He will have to come as many times as I need to impale him. We shall live until that is done."

Lord Robert was gazing down, seeking in Thomas's eyes some sense of what was to come, when Thomas threw the cloak at the torch and gave them both to darkness.   Ω

KEEP ME INFORMED

Keep me informed!
Do not EVER let Good News
suddenly one day, without Warning, take me
from out of the soupy black.
Such Surprises, coming on hintless,
I am apt to handle but poorly.
(I even might cry.)

With Disaster, do not worry;
I'll need no warm-ups; I'll be
SO ready — for old Reunion Times:
A quizzical nod, a *"You — again!?"*
and then we'll close together;
if not Best Friends, at least
we will have a Great Familiarity,
each with the other's ways.

We'll get along.
(We'll play!)
We always have.

—**David R. Bunch**

DADDY'S GIRL

by Charles D. Eckert

"Grandma Jo?"

"Yes, child?"

"Are elves and faeries really real?"

Alida Jo Worling smiled as she tucked the faded summer quilt around her granddaughter and chucked the little girl's chin. Janet was such a bright, inquisitive youngster, and so much like her father in many ways. Besides, Alida remembered asking her own grandmother a very similar question, oh, so long ago. *Things truly do stay the same,* Alida Jo thought, *in spite of the changes life brings.* It was comforting.

Wasn't it?

"Of course," Alida said, for that was what she had been told.

"No," said Janet, "I mean, really and truly."

Alida nodded and said: "Yes, dear."

"Then where are they?"

"All around."

"Here? Now?"

"No, child," Alida laughed, quietly. "Although they do live among us, we seldom — if ever — see them. Just as we rarely notice the tiny animals in the woods when we go walking, they usually don't want to be found."

"Why not?"

"Never thought to ask."

"I wish they would come out and play, sometimes," said Janet.

She's lonely, Alida thought. *Poor baby. With a tramp of a mother, who ran off, and a foolish young father who — like his father before him, first at Kwajalein then, finally, at Inchon — volunteered to go fight in some jungle half-way round the world, why wouldn't the child feel alone?* Grandma certainly understood. But, try as she might, Alida could not take the place of children her granddaughter's age, no matter how much love there was to give. Young couples with children were scarce in this area of town, for some complicated reason having to do with the schools. It seemed the neighborhood contained only a few elderly people, like herself, living out the remainder of their lives in the gingerbread houses of another time.

There was nothing to be done about any of it.

Alida had enjoyed all the old stories so much as a child that she had not considered the possibility Janet might take them **too** seriously. Yet Alida had grown up in a more simple era. Kids were exposed to such awful things, anymore. So, when she heard her granddaughter wanting to conjure playmates out of the cold realm of the Brothers Grimm, it disturbed her on a level she hadn't felt in years.

Children will believe the people they love and trust, Grandma mused, *in as much as their knowledge of the world is new and untested. They want to believe us. It's important to them.*

But a child's trust is such a fragile thing.

"I know," Alida said, bending down and kissing Janet's forehead. "But what do we need with any old elves or faeries when we have each other? Love you, Janet."

"I love you, too, Grandma," the girl said, sitting up in bed and giving Alida the best hug any grandmother could want.

"Besides," Alida went on, "you can't have faeries and elves without trolls and goblins."

"You can't?"

"Oh, no. And they can be very unpleasant creatures."

"How come?"

"Humans see the world in the light, by the sun. Goblins see the world in the dark, by the moon. That makes them think, feel, and act differently from us. In fact, we wouldn't enjoy their idea of fun at all."

"But —"

"I think I know what your next question will be," Alida said. "But before you ask, I want you to promise me you'll go right to sleep after I answer. Promise?"

"I promise."

"By the way," Alida Jo Worling said, "the answer will be our secret, just between you and me. Have you got that?"

"Yeah," Janet said, giggling. "I've got it."

———·———

"I've got it!" Jimmy yelled.

An off-white ball, scuffed and grass-stained, dropped noiselessly out of the sun as the laboring ten-year-old ran and stretched to snag it. The spheroid thunked solidly into the Wilson fielder's glove. Nearly botching the change-over, the boy managed to cock his arm and throw to second base with a practiced follow-through.

"Safe!" the umpire said.

"Good job, Jimmy," his mother called. "Nice throw!"

He waved to her and again took up his position in center field, joyfully thumping a diminutive fist into the well-oiled deep pocket of his mitt.

Janet Worling watched her son shading his eyes against the early evening dusk. As she tucked the tail of her T-shirt ("One Tough Mother") into the waistband of her Levis, she knocked her cleats against the base of the wire backstop, dislodging a few bits of moist turf. Coaching, she had discovered, was a totally unappreciated, thankless job, subject to ardent second-guessing by every parent in the stands. But it was fun, she admitted, wiping perspiration from her forehead and replacing her cap. It was also work. Who said a woman couldn't coach a baseball team? True, she hadn't known much at the beginning. But Janet had learned. She worked hard. It seemed she had to work hard, or harder, at nearly everything.

"This is WICR Radio News, at six . . ."

Over the drone of voices, the crunch of ice in portable coolers, the snick of aluminum pop-tops and the incidental yawp of a family dog, confounding and mellifluous aromas of the last straggling days of summer drifted through the woodlands at the edge of the city and across the cleared expanses of the park.

It was a fragrance of memory.

Janet would never forget Grandma Jo's old two-storey white frame house on Mercier Avenue, with its gables and grill-work, antiques and featherbeds, the varnished oak banister that dared her to slide, and the deliciously forever smells of cinnamon apples and clean linen. Those summers were spent with lavender soap in the claw-foot tub and bedtime stories of faeries, elves, and goblins leaving their children on doorsteps to be raised by humans, then coming back for them, years later, in the dark of a moonless night, when everything went bump and slither. Anything was possible.

If only life flowed as refreshingly as the twilight breezes, Janet thought. *Dear Lord, wouldn't it be wonderful?*

Yet reality naturally limits choice. A single mother did what had to be done. Jimmy depended on the strength Janet had had to learn to develop. How could he count on her if she were unable to depend on herself? Job, school, her son and baseball. Janet Worling did it all because there was no one else who could, or ever would, devil a doubt.

The sides retired and her team came up to bat.

It had not been easy, any of it. The feminists never really made *that* part of it clear. Perhaps their stalwart intelligentsia, with an odd sense of collective myopia, glibly overlooked one or two salient points to avoid confronting a reality which takes no prisoners. Or maybe not. Whatever the reasons, sometimes it was not much fun being an adult. If it weren't for Jimmy, or even this dusty diamond, it might all be —

"Come on, batter!"

"Aw, she can't hit!"

Stephanie Aikens stuffed two auburn pigtails under her cap, donned a safety helmet, then stepped awkwardly into the batter's box. Janet had worked diligently with the youngster. She remembered what it had been like for her: to be left out just for being female. Janet was determined it would not happen to this little girl.

"Strike one!" said the umpire.

The boys on the bench had not wanted Stephanie on the team, or anywhere near it, for that matter. And they didn't like her, now. When Stephanie first appeared at practice it was as though Ilse Koch had been caught weaseling through the doors of the local synagogue. It had taken every persuasive ploy in the coach's repertoire, including a well-timed threat, not only to get the girl on the team but to stave off what came close to open rebellion.

Male prejudice. It starts young. You have to stop it young.

"Strike two!"

The opposing team razzed Stephanie unmercifully. When a few members of Janet Worling's team joined in, Janet put a short order stop to it — at least on her own bench — and marveled at the ferocious invective she'd heard. Raw emotions drilled for the open like moles through soil. The boys reeked with a sweaty-male-child-smell which hung, moist and cloying, in the early evening air.

Those pre-pubescent little chauvinists, the coach thought.

And as if to confirm that conclusion Tony Alcado, the opposing pitcher, mumbled a snide, sibilant comment befitting his runty personality.

But Stephanie grinned.

Alcado shook off the first two signals from his catcher and nodded acceptance of the third. He wound up and streaked in a curve ball that caught the inside corner of home plate. Stephanie swung a clean hard cut at it and connected with the fat of the bat.

CRACK!

The ball flew off in a bullet-fast line drive, straight back at the pitcher, and caromed from the side of Alcado's head as he missed his attempt to block it with his glove. He dropped like a trophy deer.

For a moment, no one moved. Then both benches cleared. Fast. Everyone surged out to the pitcher's mound and encircled the rag-doll form of a young boy who appeared comatose.

The umpire was a paramedic, thank God, and knew what to do. He and another para, who happened to be in the bleachers, scrounged a flat board, immobilized the boy's head with a leather belt, and carried him off the field. The Volunteer Fire Department then drove Tony Alcado and his parents to County General, with blue lights flashing and dancing shadows fleeing down the winding road.

As order was restored, Janet looked around for Stephanie. A pressing urge to comfort a devastated child overwhelmed her. And the coach found her player standing casually on first base, as if that were the only place in the world to be.

"Are you all right?" said Janet.

"Sure," Stephanie said. "That was neat, huh?"

"No," the coach said, "it isn't 'neat.' "

"What do you mean?"

"Tony's hurt and we don't know how badly."

"He deserved it," said Stephanie, shrugging. "They all do."

"You can't be serious."

"Sometimes I don't understand you," the girl laughed impishly, sporting her best why-do-grownups-think-kids-are-so-dumb look; then with a sisterly wink said: "Boys."

"I don't believe what I'm hearing."

"They shouldn't pick on me," Stephanie said.

"Of course not," Janet admitted, her feelings torn and roiling, "but that doesn't give you any right to laugh at someone's pain. Injury isn't funny."

Stephanie turned sullen.

That was better than nothing, Janet decided, as she watched the child scuffing the toe-tips of her cleats into the dust on either side of the bag, a methodical shifting motion from one leg to the other. If Janet hadn't known otherwise, she would have thought Stephanie was bragging about what she'd done, almost as though the girl had purposely —

"Play Ball!"

There was nothing for it. Janet went back to the bench and saw her next three batters ground out, just as she'd known they would. Her team took the field again. As she watched her defense deploy, Janet realized how much Stephanie's attitude had shaken her. She didn't like to admit it, but it had. And it wasn't simply typical childish petulance. No, there was something else beneath it, a strange thing, inflexible and cold. The coach knew it. She had felt it.

Yet the accident was Murphy's Law.

The boys took it as given: if you played a sport, you risked injury. Period. They refused to wring their hands over getting hurt. But they didn't laugh at it, either. Its random teeth could extend to any one of them, at any time. And that was no subject for jokes.

One, two, three outs and her team was back in the dugout.

"Stephanie, come here."

"Yeah, coach?"

"You sit out the next inning."

"Why?" the girl whined.

"Because I said so," Janet Worling told her, hating herself for lapsing into that adult's catch-all which *she* had resented as a child. The fact that Janet wasn't sure why she'd said it bothered her as much as succumbing to it. But she'd been doing that, lately.

"That's not fair," Stephanie blubbered.

"Sue me," said the coach, snapping at the girl in exasperation. "Sit."

How do kids pout so instinctively?

Janet pondered this, scanning the narrow aisle separating bench and backstop, as Stephanie trudged to an empty spot along the rough-hewn planking and unceremoniously deposited herself. Whether it was genes or evolution, maybe some bench time would do the child good because, God knew, Janet hadn't many options left. She wondered if she had given Grandma Jo as much upset when she was Stephanie's age. Human memory is selective, she knew. Her own recollections could play her false. However, she did remember that Grandma had sat her in a corner, once or twice, and it turned out to be just what she'd needed.

Stephanie needed the same thing.

But Janet couldn't keep her out the entire game. This wasn't the Majors. The team simply did not have enough depth. Somehow, the coach knew, Stephanie was more than aware of the implications. Children were certainly more sophisticated, today, than had been Janet. Even so, how could a nine-year-old be *that* experienced?

Janet glanced over to the bench and noticed Stephanie staring at her. The child's face took on an odd expression which seemed to alter the familiar features of the girl. Her cheekbones jutting or more pronounced, the shape of the eyes had shifted impossibly, and the youngster's nostrils flared to full-fathomed holes plunging endlessly into the tiny head. The effect fled with one startled blink, while Janet quivered minutely in the trail of something grey and frigid —

"You're out!" barked the umpire.

Shifting her attention to the action on the field, Janet saw Don Risen dusting himself off and walking back to retrieve his glove. They had caught him in the hot box between second and third. As he dropped his safety helmet, Don couldn't meet the eyes of his coach.

"Sorry," he said. "I didn't think their left fielder could throw it that far."

"Okay," Janet said, nodding for him to take a seat. "Next time, you'll know."

"Right."

A blood-red sun floated, barely visible, over the cars in the lot. Still, both teams held each other scoreless. Janet sent Stephanie back in, this time at right field, and soon the bottom of the sixth drew to a close. Yet even during the frantic activity of retiring sides, Janet couldn't block out the image of Tony Alcado. She recalled the pathetic manikin, sprawled senseless over the loam of the pitcher's mound, and it twisted through her like a pulled strand of barbed wire.

That dwarfish snip of a girl didn't care, the coach thought. *The very idea of it is awful. What are her parents teaching her? Come to that, who are Stephanie's parents?*

Janet couldn't remember ever meeting them, whoever they were. But she decided to correct that oversight at the earliest and deliver a few choice syllables where they might be some benefit. At least, she had to try.

The top of the seventh arrived, the last inning.

Tommy Olsen hit a high pop-up which was calmly fielded by the opposing shortstop. Jimmy the Hotshot got a base-on-balls but was thrown out trying to steal third base after Bob Neal singled to left field.

What can you do? Janet mused. *Sometimes he was just like his father.*

Stephanie strode up to the plate.

Janet Worling was shocked by the rude, unconscionable behavior of the crowd. Every animal sound possible blended into a cacophony of grating disharmony, a strident jumble of boos, hisses, catcalls, and throaty rumbles, which spread from one end of the park to the other. And although Stephanie didn't pay any attention to it, Janet was appalled. The child's dismissal of a hostile mob was either uncommon courage or glacial indifference. Coach Worling wasn't sure. It didn't seem to make any difference, either way.

The first pitch was high, outside. Ball one.

She's still angry with me, Janet realized, *for scolding her and planting her tush on the bench.*

The coach knew it by sight, but the mother in Janet would have seen it in the dark. *Why do adults bother, in words or actions, telling children: "It's for your own good"? Because it usually is. Yet what child would believe that?*

The second pitch was low. Ball two.

Stephanie paused, dusting her hands, balancing her Louisville Slugger, adjusting her stance in the box. During this display, she glanced repeatedly at her coach. The adult's cheek pressed against the wire backstop, fingers entwined in the mesh. It was a habit of nerves and weeks of concern and worry.

Janet peered through the steel and saw something bestial, utterly bestial — vertical-irised piss-yellow eyes, lips thinned and stretched in invisibility above a mandrill's smile of prominent canines which looked dry and discolored, protruding brow ridges, taut, pallid skin — momentarily superimposed on the smooth innocent face; then nothing. The third pitch came right down the pipe and Stephanie swung.

CRACK!

The foul-tipped ball struck with *eldritch* accuracy.

Janet fell away, a wire-mesh pattern engraved on her cheek, before she knew why. Her left eye swelled immediately, as she noticed how the ground felt against the flat of her back. The first stars of evening dotted the sky.

The park was stone silent.

——— - ———

"Now, what was your question?" said Grandma Jo.

Janet thought for a moment, then spoke: "You said the faeries and goblins don't want to be found."

"That's right."

"Are they afraid?"

"Maybe so."

"Is that why they're so mean?"

Grandma Jo sat down on the edge of her granddaughter's bed. "I don't think they were always mean," she said. "But how would you feel if your kind was dwindling due to the onslaught of humans crowding onto the land you once called home? If you were an intelligent creature, you would be able to see and understand what was going on. If you had powers, yet could not reverse the approaching hordes, would you be content to remain a cute, benign forest dweller? It's likely you'd become resentful, angry, malignant and determined. And if so, would you use your powers to help you and your kind, and likewise to hinder the invader? Would you alter your true form and infiltrate whenever possible? Could you teach your children to feel no remorse for any mischief or pain they could inflict on 'the enemy'? Would you go so far as to punish compassion?"

"Mmmmmmmmmmmmmm."

"Or would you just go to sleep like my little Janet . . . ?"

——— - ———

Janet Worling slowly picked herself up off the dirt floor of the dugout. At first, she couldn't understand why the individual members of her team — even her own son, Jimmy — remained seated while they watched her progress. No one made any move to help her. Yet, as she met their nearly uniform expressions, Janet saw that she now shared a bond with her boys, a rite of passage, an initiation, a special something which had been previously denied her.

Had they always known?

Yes, the answer came back in soundless eloquence, with the pain of earned knowledge, from young male faces with very old eyes. *Now, do you understand?*

Janet Worling did, at last.

And I'm sorry, Grandma Jo, Janet thought. *I heard you when you tucked me in, late at night, but I didn't listen.*

Ignoring the pain and looking beyond her tears, Coach Worling turned towards a true Goblinchild, with auburn pigtails, who stood near home plate and was quietly chuckling behind a feral grin.

"I hope her parents come for her soon." Janet said.

Would there be no moon, tonight? Ω

THE BEDPOSTS OF LIFE

by Robert Bloch

He hated what he was doing, but he couldn't help it.

None of them could help it, because their need was too great. The great need for great sex.

Well, they wouldn't find it here. Most of them knew this in advance but still they came, night after night, cruising the street in slow-moving silence more appropriate to a funeral procession than a journey of joy. It was, perhaps, fitting that they should do so, for virtually all those who gathered here mourned the loss of love.

Some had never even known it: the very young, the shy, the awkward and unattractive victims of low self-esteem. But their need was as compelling, perhaps more so than that of the others. When you're hungry the body doesn't demand delicacies; it settles for junk-food. Young appetites value quantity over quality, and the quantity was here. *Great sex?* At this stage in their lives any sex at all was great, just so there was enough of it available.

When you're old, availability becomes a problem once again. Dirty old men get hungry too. Just because you lose your teeth doesn't mean you lose your appetite. If gourmet fare is harder to come by, there's plenty of take-outs for midnight snacks. The street is a convenience-store.

He strolled along, scanning faces crouched over steering-wheels. Along with the generation-gap's extremes were men in their prime, drivers who were themselves driven by impulse impossible to control.

For amusement he made a little game of relating cars to their occupants. The lone-some Audi, stranger in town. Slinky-styled old Bugatti on the prowl for young meat. That dented white Ford wagon conjured up the image of a harried, housebroken middle-aging husband whose spouse selected the vehicle as a convenience for hauling kids. He'd borrowed it to come here in temporary escape from the bonds of unholy matrimony.

Bonds. *Bondage.* That van with the drawn window-curtains — did they conceal contents, cords and cuffs and chains so dearly beloved in sado-masochistic union? One could never be sure, it was all guesswork, really. That old Chevy truck spewing exhaust might have a driver wearing pantyhose under his jeans. This Mercedes might be owned by a substantial stockbroker, or some swinging substance-abuser. And driving a Porsche doesn't guarantee your potency. Wherefore art thou, Alfa-Romeo?

He shrugged the thought aside. It was time to stop searching the street and turn his attention to the sidewalk.

That's where the women waited: the hookers, the hustlers, the broads and the bimbos.

The women were like cars, in a way. Big or small, wide-bodied or compact, flashy models with fresh paint-jobs, old pickups beyond repair. None were brand-new, but when you're looking for a used car you've got to expect some mileage on it. In a case like this you weren't even buying, just picking a rental. And design wasn't as important as locating a comfortable, trouble-free ride.

Never mind the colors, either. He noted a little yellow one, probably a Japanese import, but there was a wide selection in white, black or brown. No sticker-prices, all that was a matter of bargaining, so he might as well be guided by the mood of the moment and indulge his whim.

Just what was his whim in women this evening?

How about that brassy blonde in the miniskirt riding up almost to her thighs? He watched as she strutted along the edge of the walk near the curb, eyeing the drivers and giving them an eyeful. Not his type, he decided. Not tonight, Josephine.

Hadn't heard anyone say that in years. *Not tonight, Josephine.* Now there was an oldie for you. A golden oldie, like the blonde, whose ravaged countenance was clearly and cruelly revealed as she came closer.

He avoided her glance, fixing his attention on the dark-haired girl who stood under a doorway, half in shadow, like a Rembrandt portrait. But there the resemblance ended. When she moved forward into the street he saw what shadow had partially concealed; the body of a woman, the face of a child, the eyes of a whore.

He hurried past her, then shrugged as he continued at a slower pace, reminding himself again that variations in age, build or complexion were unimportant. One size fits all. What difference did it make which woman he chose?

The answer stood on the corner, under the stoplight.

The light was orange. The smooth bare skin of her arms and shoulders was orange too.

The light was red. Her helmet of hair was red too.

The light was green. Under their long lashes, the eyes that stared at him were green.

Colorful. Changeable. And all illusion. Still, it added an element of diversion which might make things just a trifle easier. He didn't like what he was going to do, but that couldn't be helped. And

after all, she was only a whore.

So the time had come to make his move. To walk slow and easy, talk slow and easy. Big smile now, that's the trick.

"Good evening," he said.

When the trick said hello she knew he was the one. She didn't like what she was going to do, but a girl has to eat. And after all, he was only a John.

Not a bad-looking one, either, she decided. Tall, dark and handsome, like they used to say in those late-night reruns of old movies. Regular movies, that is, not like the kind you got in motels. God, how many of those lousy porno flicks had she sat through? And why did so many Johns need them to turn on with? No wonder they had problems making it with the wife or girlfriend. But hey, don't knock it, if they didn't have problems she'd be out of business. And right now she needed business, needed it bad because of the way things had been going lately. But to Hell with *lately,* this is *now.* No yesterday, no tomorrow.

She flashed on all this while she was talking to the John, fast-talking, sweet-talking, double-talking, the same line she always handed out upfront to stall for time.

Thing is, you needed time to size up a trick before the deal went down. Maybe in the old days it was easier to go by appearances, like the kind of clothes a John wore. But now everybody tried to look like a slob, so you had to check out details; kind of shoes he had on, did he wear a drugstore watch or a good one, was there dirt under his nails?

Sometimes you could get a fix on the kind of car they drove, but a lot of creeps switched to some old junker when they had to purge the urge. Old cars and old clothes helped them poormouth you over the price, so it was up to you to spot phonies. Because the price was same as always — whatever the traffic would bear.

Only this John didn't come with the traffic, not unless he was one of the real smartasses who parked down a side street and walked the rest of the way. Or maybe he'd come out of some motel around here, except he didn't look like the type who'd be staying in these roach-ranches. No tie, but wool dress slacks and a dark jacket; shirt underneath longsleeved, because the cuffs showed. Leather shoes, too, oxfords instead of those plastic slip-ons.

Everything added up — added up to maybe twenty, thirty dollars more than regular, plus a kickback from the motel if he didn't have a flop of his own. She didn't have a main man to look out for her now, so she'd damn well better look out for herself. Don't go off the turf with a trick, don't cab to his pad. Keep cool, fool.

No problem. Turned out all he wanted was great sex, nothing kinky, no side-order of fries. The price she set didn't seem to bother him and yes, he'd pay upfront, soon as they registered. He left it to her to pick out a place, which is why the two of them ended up in that neat suite at the C'mon Inn.

The open closet space had four of those goddam hangers that don't come off the rack, the curtains smelled of stale smoke, and the bed-lamp was broken, but no problem.

And no problem with the money. All in twenties, she noticed, it came out of a fancy billfold with a zipper. Initials stamped on in gold lettering but she couldn't make them out because the bulb in the corner floor-lamp was too dim. And when he turned it off the only light came from outside the window where the neon sign flickered on and off. Off was black, on was blue, black and blue, jerk better not try beating on her, no S&M, just straight, right?

But he didn't get out of line, just waited as she peeled her things off and stood beside the bed, first a black blur, then a bright blue body with burnished blue hair, blazing blue eyes.

He glanced up at her as he shed his clothes. "Blue angel," he said.

"What?"

The Blue Angel." He pulled her down beside him. "Old movie. Saw it in Germany when it first came out. Before your time."

She ran her eyes and hands over his lean, muscular frame. "Don't con me. You aren't all that old."

"And you're not that much of an angel. Appearances can be deceptive." He chuckled as if what he'd just said was funny, but it wasn't.

A frown creased her forehead and she creased it out quickly. But she might have known what to expect; these neat dressers were always the ones, talk your ear off if you let them. Okay, so she got paid to let them, only she didn't have to like it. If it's talk they wanted, why not spend their dough on phone-calls. Talk is for singles-bars. Way we do business here, buddy, is get it up, get it over with, and get out. That's how she liked it.

Only she didn't like it. And she hated him, hated all of them, talk or no talk. If it wasn't for one of them she wouldn't be here, but too late to worry about that now, all she could do was hate the whole stinking dirty lot —

"What are you thinking about?" he said.

"Nothing."

He smiled. "Man's question. Woman's answer."

Now he bent forward, searching her face, and his smile faded. Outside the window the neon eye blinked at them, its light sweeping over the moon of flesh suspended above her, searching minute craters and crevasses. Maybe he was older than she'd figured.

That part didn't bother her, but she was starting to feel a little edgy about the way he looked when he wasn't smiling. Those eyes of his were something else — every time the neon switched on he was staring at her, staring into her, deep, as if he could read her mind.

"Don't worry," she told him. "I'm okay."

"No you're not." His smile came back, but it was different now, like his voice; it belonged in the dark, not the flashing blue light. "You wish you weren't here, don't you?"

He *was* reading her mind! She couldn't find a smile for him now, and it was hard to even manage a voice. "I'm okay, I tell you."

"Don't lie to me," he said. "And I won't lie to you." He was staring, staring right through her. "If it's any consolation, I don't want to be here either. But at the moment, there's little choice." His voice deepened, and so did the blue flame in his eyes. "Like everyone else, my dear, there are times when our need takes us prisoner. We are all tied to the bedposts of life."

She felt his hatred then, just as he must feel hers, and it was in hatred now that they moved through the mimicry of love. It seemed to her that the light flashed on and off at a faster tempo in unison with their own.

There was no smile looming above her now and no frown, just the feral savagery of flaring nostrils and bared teeth as he rasped in rut. She closed her eyes to shut out the sight but she couldn't shield herself from sensation, and when he merged pain with pleasure her eyes went wide for a moment, then clamped shut as her head fell back into darkness unbroken by fitful neon glare.

How long she lay there she didn't know, but when at last her eyes opened again and awareness came, he was gone.

No trace of pleasure remained, but with the coming of awareness, pain returned. Involuntarily her fingers rose to graze across her throat and came away stained with a trickle of bluish ooze in the momentary flicker of light.

Blood. That's what it was. The old John had bitten her in the neck. And now she remembered when it had happened, when she felt the pain and opened her eyes and the blue light winked on and she stared up over his shoulder at the dressing-table on the far side of the room to see herself as she lay there on the bed. Lay there alone, because he cast no reflection in the mirror.

She'd blacked out from shock then, but at the recollection she started to laugh and couldn't stop; it felt as though she'd never stop until she was dead. Only now she would never die, any more than he could. And both of them would share their pain forever.

He, of course, was a vampire.

And she had AIDS.   Ω

WEIRD TALES TALKS WITH RAMSEY CAMPBELL

by Stephen Jones

Weird Tales: You had a very strange childhood . . . ?

Ramsey Campbell: Yes, my parents were estranged very early — I was conceived, I think three months after they got married, and by the time I was born the marriage had pretty much come apart. But because this was the 1950s, and because my mother was a Catholic, they nevertheless continued to live in the same house.

It was a pretty small house by contemporary standards, with two rooms downstairs and three bedrooms. We all lived together, although my parents were very quickly not on speaking terms; some of the first things I remember are them having violent arguments and soon after that I became a sort of messenger who had to go over and say, "My mother says this . . ." and "Will you ask your father this . . ."

However, shortly it grew more extreme than that and my father, although continuing to live in the same house, simply became an invisible presence. He came in at night and he went out in the morning, but I didn't see him face-to-face for virtually twenty years. When I got older and was going out to work or going to the movies, if we should encounter each other he would actually hold the door closed from the other side so that we couldn't come face-to-face. For whatever reason, I don't know, and I never got the chance to ask him.

The other side of all this was that my mother was clinically schizophrenic and, although I didn't have the words for it then, it certainly became increasingly clear to me at a very early age that there were things that she perceived which were not as I perceived them, and on the whole I was probably right!

WT: So because of this bizarre family background, were you a very isolated child?

Campbell: I was a pretty isolated child, yes. However, children are extraordinarily resilient; and, as far as you're concerned at that age, this is how childhood is. You don't really notice that it's not how other people conduct their childhood until later on.

I was very introverted and moderately withdrawn, though I had a fair number of friends at school, but I read a lot and this would have happened anyway. I started reading at a very early age.

I read pretty well anything I could get my hands on, initially children's fiction, obviously. I would have been five — no more than six I'm sure — and we were passing a newsagent's window when I saw an issue of *Weird Tales* and I remember thinking, "I want this." Specifically, I remember seeing the image on the cover and what it appeared to me to depict was a kind of birdlike creature in the foreground in a state of extreme panic and, across what appeared to be a black desert, these two creatures like glowing skeletons with very large skulls and impossibly small bodies were coming towards it for probably extremely evil intent.

This image stuck in my mind for years and years. It must have been at least ten years later when I finally tracked down the issue concerned (the November 1952 issue). What it actually turned out to show was some bones in a desert with the vultures perched on them and two skeletons in the background. That's all it was, but somehow my seeing that cover in the window was the point at which I started to imagine, actually to create horror fiction, if you like; I wasn't writing it down yet, but it seems to me the process began right there.

WT: When did you begin collecting books and magazines?

Campbell: When I was ten I was actually allowed to begin collecting *Weird Tales* and other magazines, and I remember reading the letter columns and there would be all these titles which I found immensely exciting and which invoked enormous kinds of vague but extraordinary imaginative visions which I then wanted to go out and buy.

I used to look at the Arkham House ads for things like *The Opener of the Way* and *The Hounds of Tindalos* and *The Abominations of Yondo* and I eventually discovered that Arkham House was still going, and began to collect their books as well.

WT: When did you begin writing your own stories, and did you receive encouragement from anyone else?

Campbell: Pretty soon after going to secondary school, probably just to impress the English teacher, I brought in some samples of the stuff I was writing. I was now actually completing short stories but they were dire, believe me! Everything was just stuck together end-to-end with very little relevance other than here was a bit of a monster, here was a bit that might fit as the climax. There was an extended — well, extended for my age then, about six thousand words maybe — pastiche of Dennis Wheatley, particularly the Wheatley of *The Devil Rides Out.*

I was just imitating everything in sight; but nevertheless I brought some of these hand-written stories into school; and, to his credit, the English master (who was one of the Christian Brothers who ran the school) was sort of impressed and actually persuaded me to read the stuff out to the class.

Well, I didn't need any particular encouragement to do that! These stories became the very first collection that I finished when I was just about twelve years old — it's called *Ghostly Tales,* and Bob Price actually published it a couple of years ago.

I suppose at least a few of those stories, for all their faults, do have some narrative sense and don't seem to make too many of the obvious structural errors which you find in that sort of early writing — where the writer either takes too much time over the redundant detail or rushes at the story so fast that all the significant detail never gets put in. Bad and derivative as they are, at least they've got a certain instinct for storytelling.

So I floundered on, when, very shortly after this, I got my first H.P. Lovecraft collection. This was the British edition of the Avon paperback *The Lurking Fear,* known as *Cry Horror!* in Britain. I found a single copy in a newsagent's a couple of miles away from home.

I grabbed it, and remember I couldn't stand the thought of having this thing sitting at home waiting to be read. I wanted to read it *now,* so I pretended to be ill and took the day off school, and I just sat there and read it from cover to cover. This day of reading Lovecraft convinced me that he was not only the greatest horror writer I'd ever read, but he was absolutely the greatest *writer* I'd ever read, and that this was the model I wanted to follow, which I duly did.

WT: When did you first begin corresponding with August Derleth at Arkham House?

Campbell: I would have been just about fifteen. In so far as Derleth was Lovecraft's publisher, and since my stories were very clearly imitation Lovecraft, a correspondent suggested I send them off to him and see what he made of them. I don't think I was honestly expecting much more than he might say "These are bad." In fact he sent me back a two-page single-spaced letter going into enormous detail about precisely what was wrong with all this stuff and how bad much of it was. Then he ended by saying "They need a lot of work, but this may well be a potential Arkham House book." Pretty strong stuff to get when you're fifteen years old! So I got an editor's input very early in my career, which was ideal.

WT: What was your first professional sale?

Campbell: My first professional sale was to Derleth. It was a story called "The Church in High Street," which was very much imitation Lovecraft, and it was published in *Dark Mind, Dark Heart* in 1962. Derleth re-wrote it to some extent — he accepted it on the basis that he had a free hand to re-work it as he saw fit. I think this was perfectly valid, I mean, he was actually showing me how to do it, although there are things in it which I'd do differently if I were re-writing it now. So here I was in print alongside Robert Bloch and John Metcalfe and H. Russell Wakefield.

WT: Had you any thoughts at this time of becoming a full-time writer?

Campbell: Derleth recommended me strongly not to try to write full-time, which he clearly felt to some extent had been his own downfall. He suggested I get some kind of steady job which wouldn't be too demanding outside work hours so I could take time to write. So I left school when I was sixteen and went into the Civil Service for four years, then I switched to the Public Libraries for another seven years.

WT: How did your first collection, *The Inhabitant of the Lake and Less Welcome Tenants,* come to be published?

Campbell: Well, it was basically the stuff I was writing under Derleth's tuition. I pulled "The Church in High Street" out because he'd said he was doing this anthology and he wanted a story for it. It was clear from the way he introduced the story that it was a way of getting my name in front of his audience because he was already talking about the first collection being in preparation. I completed *The Inhabitant of the Lake* when I was seventeen and it came out in 1964. I had already begun to learn a fair amount from Derleth's tuition, I was doing things like allowing the characters to develop a little, lots more dialogue than Lovecraft would have used — not that the dialogue was necessarily any good.

WT: Did Derleth revise many of the stories in the book?

Campbell: Well, I think he changed the odd word, a couple of bits of strong language which he didn't think fitted, and I think he was right — in a Lovecraft pastiche it doesn't. But otherwise he left it virtually untouched.

WT: What was your reaction when you saw a copy of your first book?

Campbell: Amazement, obviously. It was astonishing really. Here was an actual Arkham House book with my name on it! It had particular significance for me, after all I'd read all those Arkham ads and to some extent I'd tried to make the titles have that sort of resonance, you know — "The Inhabitant of the Lake," "The Horror from the Bridge" — the sort of thing that you might have read in a *Weird Tales* ad and thought, "Yeah, I've got to read that just for the title."

WT: With your first hardcover collection published in America, did you have any thoughts about seeing your work in print in Britain?

Campbell: No, I didn't. I felt about Arkham House very much the way Lovecraft felt about *Weird Tales* — that it was my only market. I even felt that if I started selling stories to other markets maybe Derleth wouldn't want to use them in a collection, which of course wouldn't have necessarily been true. I really did have this tunnel vision about markets for a long time, and it wasn't until Robert Lowndes wrote an editorial in *Magazine of Horror,* reviewing a Derleth anthology, *Travellers By Night,* and singled my first Liverpool story — "The Cellars" — out at considerable length, that I thought, "My God, here's somebody who actually likes my stuff, I've got to send him something." Which I did.

My first professional British contact was Richard Davis, who was the story editor on a BBC horror show which lasted for one series. So what he did was bring out an anthology of stories he would have bought if there had been a second series, and he bought two of mine — "Reply Guaranteed" and "The Stocking" — and that was my first British sale. I was beginning to see that maybe it was possible to submit to other markets as well as Arkham House.

WT: Were you particularly prolific during this early period of your writing career?

Campbell: It's probably worth pointing out that *Demons by Daylight,* which I began work on not long after *The Inhabitant of the Lake,* actually took me five years to write. This was because I'd spent something like two-and-a-half years writing the first drafts of many of the stories, became extremely dissatisfied with them and used the first drafts as a model of how not to do it and started again.

I'd gone through a period of extreme dissatisfaction with the entire field. I'd now begun to read considerably outside it — Iris Murdoch, Graham Greene, Lawrence Durrell, Malcolm Lowry, Samuel Beckett and so on — and I felt there was this whole body of literature out there which had concerns which somehow were not being reflected in horror.

It seemed to me, why *can't* horror talk about these things as well? So I spent five years trying to do it, and I must say there were many times when I thought, "Hang on, if nobody else is doing this doesn't that mean that maybe they're right and I'm wrong?" So I was really out in the dark by myself.

WT: What was the initial reaction like to your second collection?

Campbell: *Demons by Daylight* should have come out in 1971, but Derleth died and it was put back two years. I never really knew what he thought of it. He sent me a contract, which obviously meant he thought *something,* but he never actually wrote to tell me his feelings about the book. I suspect it wasn't absolutely to his taste.

Derleth did write the note in the Arkham catalogue which said, basically, "this book gives adequate proof of the writer's creative growth" — a pretty guarded statement when you think about it!

I remember an enormously long — I would think ten thousand words — exegesis in Harry Morris's fanzine *Nyctalops* by T.E.D. Klein. Everything I wanted to be in the book was there in his account, so clearly I was communicating with *somebody.* So on the basis of two short-story collections in print and one extremely intelligent essay about the second book, I decided this was enough to chuck up my job in the library and go full-time, which I did in mid-1973.

WT: Were you getting encouragement from anyone?

Campbell: I was married by this time, and Jenny was extremely encouraging. I also received the occasional letter from Robert Bloch, who has always been very encouraging, not just to me, but to young writers generally.

I was also in touch with Kirby McCauley, who'd begun corresponding with me from my very first story back in 1962 when he was a Sears Roebuck salesman. Basically he would just write to anyone whose work he admired and send them immensely long letters in longhand. We also discovered we had other things in common, like music and cinema.

Then Kirby decided he was going to become an agent. He was corresponding with Basil Copper and Robert Aickman and other writers in Britain, and he'd noted that they didn't have an American agent so he thought, "I'll be it." He gave up his job and moved to New York and basically went around all the publishers making himself known. So I now had an agent in America.

Kirby had been saying gently but frequently, "You've got to write a novel" — I'd been writing short stories and nothing else for thirteen years, but gradually into my consciousness did percolate this notion that maybe I really should write a novel; before any professional publication I'd had a go at writing novels but never finished them. So in 1976 I'd got enough of an idea together, enough material for it, and I simply got up one morning and wrote the first line.

WT: How long did it take to complete *The Doll Who Ate His Mother*?

Campbell: It took about six months, I suppose. I always do the first draft in longhand in old standard exercise books with spiral binding. I leave the lefthand page blank and write on the righthand page so I've got the space on the left to do any immediate revisions.

WT: Did you have to do many drafts of the book?

Campbell: Not that many, partly because so much of the work had gone into gathering the material and actually plotting the chapters. When I got to sitting down to write the book, most of it was already in there waiting to be written; and of course there was other stuff that I hadn't conceived which began to spill out which I think is the good stuff about the book. It was pretty much one draft really.

WT: Was there anything about *The Doll That Ate His Mother* that disappointed you?

Campbell: There are always things about a book that disappoint you, it's always going to be the next book that's going to be the one you're reaching for; but precisely because you continue to reach I suppose is why you continue to write.

WT: Your second novel, *The Face That Must Die*, is amongst your bleakest work. Why is that?

Campbell: I'd been doing some stories in which autobiographical elements had begun to surface — "The Chimney" is a particular example where, in many ways, the story is about the fact that I used to have to go out every Christmas Day and knock on my father's door and say, "Are you coming down for Christmas lunch?" And when there was no answer I used to scuttle back downstairs and think, "Thank God that's over for another year!" In the story it's specifically about a child who is terrified of what comes down the chimney on Christmas Eve, which turns out to be, in some sense, his father. So I don't think you need to look too far for a basis for that story. Though I have to say that when I was writing it, I wasn't aware that that was what I was writing about: it was just this story about this character in this situation.

In *The Face That Must Die* there is no doubt that I was, to some extent, using autobiographical material more consciously, specifically that my mother was convinced that she often passed people on the street whom she would mistake for film actors, and not infrequently she would see newspaper identikit pictures of criminals and would say, "I know that face." I did feel she might go up to somebody on the street and say, "You are the man," and it occurred to me, "Well, all right, supposing this really did happen, what would happen next?"

Or supposing the person convinced of this then became convinced that everybody was conspiring to cover up on behalf of this other person, who was in fact not the culprit at all. Where would we go from there?

This is basically where the novel goes. What I wanted to do in the story, and what I think is the source of most of its power, is that it actually places you inside the head of that character for chapters on end, something that some people still find very hard to take.

WT: I believe you had problems selling it . . . ?

Campbell: Several companies said, "We can't publish this." One of the guys who rejected the book on the basis that it was too bleak was Thomas Tessier, when he was the editor at Millington in London. Later on, when the book came out in America, they restored the complete version because when it was published in Britain the first edition was somewhat cut.

WT: For what reasons?

Campbell: I took out one chapter because I thought it didn't advance the narrative particularly and it also seemed to make the book even more unsympathetic than it already was.

By this time I'd reached such a stage of despondency about the thing that the fact that it was going into print in some version was enough.

WT: By the mid-1970s the novels began to take precedence over your prolific output of short stories. Was this because the financial benefits were so much greater?

Campbell: Well, there was a bit of that, certainly. Having said that, *The Face That Must Die* was regarded by everyone who looked at it — apart from Star Books — as being too grim to publish. It also has to be said that *The Doll Who Ate His Mother* did extremely badly in its first edition.

Something had to be done, so for the first and only time I actually tried to conceive a novel which was what I thought the market wanted, which was *The Parasite* (*To Wake the Dead* in Britain). I tried to do what appeared to be the perceived model of the contemporary horror story, which is characters in an ordinary environment and something *out there* is attempting to get them for whatever reason.

Now I have to say that it didn't quite come off that way. The story is still about someone whose dormant male personality overtakes her and pushes her in increasingly disturbing directions, so it still becomes a psychological horror novel, but I don't think it can be read very seriously as that. It is mostly a horror novel which just huffs and puffs and tries to be as horrible and loathsome and scary as possible. It's got a few good things in it, but . . .

WT: But it achieved the desired effect, didn't it?

Campbell: Yes it did — it got reviews, not all of which by any means were favourable, but at least it got them. And it certainly got sales — the paperback took off quite considerably.

I took about forty thousand words out of the first draft of *The Parasite* because it was much too long, and I did all that cutting myself. Having learned how to do that, I was then considerably more succinct in *The Nameless*, which followed.

It's odd, because that book looks in retrospect as if it's been conceived as a fairly fast, slick horror thriller; what it really was was simply that our daughter Tammy had been born and I got the sort of parental horrors about what happens if your child is stolen. Presumably the techniques I was beginning to learn were a lot more flexible.

WT: Since then you've written *Incarnate, Obsession, The Hungry Moon, The Influence, Ancient Images* and *Midnight Sun.* Do you aim to produce a novel per year?

Campbell: Less than that, probably every eighteen months perhaps. Whereas I used to plot very thoroughly, now I don't. Generally speaking, I'll go with the book once I know who the characters are, what they do, and to some extent what the situation is. Then I'll start writing, and whereas all the struggling, not merely to shape the material but actually to find out what it is, used to be before I started writing the novel, now it's in the process of writing it. I always revise on the keyboard and the really enjoyable part becomes the re-write: where I can actually look at what took me a day or two to write and say, "Fine, I need two sentences out of this and the rest of it can go." That gives me intense pleasure — clarifying, trying to make the writing clearer; I've got a lot more fond of that than I used to be.

WT: Do you attempt to write for a market, and is there much editorial interference from your publishers?

Campbell: No, I write just what pleases me. I must admit that it's odd, because I keep expecting more editorial interference. You actually send your book off to them and think, "Christ, this is awful; even if it's any good they're not going to like it because it clearly is not what I did last time." Actually this may not be true: in a sense, the more you try not to repeat yourself, in a peculiar way the more you are true to yourself as a writer.

WT: There are obviously certain themes that run through all your work; are you aware of them while you are writing?

Campbell: Sometimes I am, in which case I try to avoid them. If I find I've done this before then I actually try either to suppress the scene or at least take it in a new direction. *Midnight Sun* is an attempt to do a visionary horror novel, more in the Algernon Blackwood tradition or the subtler side of Lovecraft, and I thought I was trying to do this at novel length for the first time. But when I looked back at *The Parasite* I realised that in fact that is what I'd been trying to do there as well.

I think it's a lot more successful in *Midnight Sun*. That was the most hell-ish book yet: fifteen months in the writing and I had weeks thinking, "My God, why am I doing this? What's the point?" There was just that light at the end of the tunnel which made me think, "Okay, I've just got to try and continue reaching there." When I'd finished it I actually did think it was a reasonably successful attempt at a novel which is terrifying and awesome rather than physically violent. There's virtually no physical violence in the entire book.

WT: Have you ever considered leaving the horror genre behind altogether?

Campbell: Unless *Midnight Sun* is a mainstream book, or unless my novella *Needing Ghosts* is a mainstream story, I don't personally care. The definitions don't really matter to me. As far as I'm concerned, I'm writing horror fiction but I don't mind what anyone else calls it. I'm going to say I write horror fiction because that's what I think I do.

WT: Although you've been a published horror writer for almost thirty years, your work has never quite achieved the mass appeal of, say, Stephen King or Dean R. Koontz, nor the commercial rewards that go with that type of popularity. Does this perhaps make you resentful?

Campbell: I don't know about resentful, but the one thing I regret so far (things can change, obviously) is the sense that there is an audience out there which would like what I'm doing and doesn't know about it. It does bother me, but I don't quite know how one gets to that audience.

I do a lot of readings; one of the things I particularly enjoy is reading to audiences. Quite often I get people coming up at the end saying, "Well, we didn't realize people were writing this kind of horror anymore," and that is the kind of audience I would like to reach.

Peter Ackroyd's doing it of course, and maybe Susan Hill. But there seems to be this peculiar thing whereby somebody — not necessarily from outside the field, but who gets packaged as if they are — has to sound the death knell for the genre in order for somebody else to come along and claim to have resuscitated it. I do think that whole audiences out there need to be alerted to what the field itself has been achieving, but how you do it I don't know. I think we're picking them up gradually.

WT: So, of your own work, which is your personal favorite?

Campbell: Well, we have a slight problem here as it's fairly common to think your last story is your best. I certainly think *Midnight Sun* is about as well as I've done that sort of tale of supernatural terror, and I suppose it's an attempt to do at greater length what I did in my short story, "The Voice of the Beach" — which I think is the one story in which I managed to get close to what I feel Lovecraft achieved, or as close as I'm likely to come. I suppose that's a favourite in a way, too.

Also *The Face That Must Die* because it's relentless and it doesn't mess around. No matter how technically clumsy it is in some ways, at least it doesn't compromise in any way, and I

quite like that.

WT: Where do you see your career going from here?

Campbell: The serious answer is I've absolutely no idea, and that's the good part, isn't it?

I've got piles of notebooks and piles of notes in the books for ideas which I haven't yet used. Some of them may never get used.

The great excitement is precisely that you don't know what you are going to do five years from now. I mean, I know that the next book I'll do is a psychological horror novel with no supernatural element, *The Count of Eleven*, but beyond that . . . I think I've got an idea of what the novel after that *might* be but then of course, between then and now, something else may have suggested itself to me.

WT: Do you think you are still learning your craft as a horror writer?

Campbell: Oh, probably, but I think I'd cut off your question even earlier than that. I think I'm still learning my *craft*. I think you always continue to do that — it's a learning experience, which is exactly what makes it all so appealing.
Ω

THE SHAPE OF THRILLS TO COME!

In *Weird Tales*® 302, the special William F. Nolan issue, we have new fiction by Nolan, Ronald Anthony Cross, and Brian Lumley.

And in *Weird Tales*® 303, our featured author is Thomas Ligotti, with additional stories by Keith Taylor and William Wu.

Weird Tales® 304 will be a John Brunner issue, with his "Concerning the Forthcoming Inexpensive Paperback Translation of the Necronomicon of Abdul Alhazred" and other stories.

Appearing soon: stories by S.P. Somtow, Steve Rasnic Tem, Tanith Lee, and Darrell Schweitzer, along with more poetry by Robert E. Howard and Ray Bradbury.

GROWING UP

by John R. Little

Harry Selkirk was 33 years old before he realized that something was missing. Not that he was missing much, mind you — he was a successful chartered accountant, and nobody could miss the twinkle in Old Man Kolfax's eye when he watched Harry. He would be made the next partner of the firm.

Harry owned a silver BMW and lived in a huge ranch-style house in North Vancouver overlooking the Pacific. Although the house was mostly owned by his bank, Harry did own outright a modest cottage in the interior, where he faithfully spent three weeks each summer, fishing and enjoying the quiet.

But on his 33rd birthday, he had a revelation so clear it jolted him awake at 6 A.M., an hour earlier than normal.

Harry wanted to have a son.

Not a daughter and not even a wife, although she would likely come with the package, but a son. Harry could remember his mother's overpowering voice booming when he had left home. "Gotta get yourself married, boy. Get yourself some kids. They'll keep you young at heart for the rest of your days."

Well, Harry thought. *I don't know about that*. But he did know he wanted a son.

Harry had rarely dated women. When he was fifteen, he had charted out his own future carefully, culminating with his own accounting firm by the time he was forty. So far, everything was dead on track, and it irked him that he hadn't thought enough to put a son into the plans.

As he was shaving, Harry ran through the possibilities. He could afford to hire a woman for a year to bear his son, but that seemed a bit too crass.

He could adopt, but that wouldn't be right, either; he needed a boy that carried his genes.

There didn't seem to be many other alternatives: he would have to get married.

He cut himself with his razor as he realized this. *Damn*, he thought. *Who would want to marry me?*

The question remained unanswered until he went to work that morning and said hello to Cathy, the office receptionist.

"Hi," she answered.

Harry was about to walk past her into his office when he looked back at her more closely. Pretty, more or less. Nice personality. "Would you be interested in dinner tonight?" he asked.

Harry and Cathy were married three months later. Harry woke up the day after with a smile on his face. He knew that Cathy was now carrying his son.

Nine months later, on Harry's thirty-fourth birthday, Harry Selkirk, Jr., was born.

Harry, Sr., doted on the baby to the exclusion of all else. He immediately took his three weeks' holiday to play with baby Harry, spending every minute with him. He wouldn't allow Cathy to breast-feed the baby, since that would take him away from his father for fifteen minutes at a time.

It was Hell for Harry to finish his holidays. He phoned in sick with a fictitious flu to add an extra week with the child, but after that he ran out of excuses and had to go back to the office.

"Babies must agree with you," said Old Man Kolfax when Harry showed up at the accounting firm. "You look great."

"They say kids keep you young," said Harry.

For six months, Harry dreaded nighttime, since that meant morning would soon come, and he would have to leave Junior for eight straight hours to go to work.

Cathy grew more and more frustrated and soon gave up and left Harry. She had been totally ignored since the baby was born and just wanted to get away. Harry didn't try to stop her, but rather encouraged her to leave. He went in to work the next day with Junior in his arms and smiled as he handed a neatly-typed resignation letter to Kolfax.

"You can't leave," said Kolfax in disbelief. "We were about to promote you."

Harry knew he had to leave. People would soon begin to notice too much. "Sorry," he said. "I've got more important things on my mind."

"But what about your papers and —"

"Help yourself to whatever you like. So long."

Harry stopped at the first realtor that he saw and asked them to sell his house as soon as possible. They scrambled to find a buyer a week later, and Harry made a thirty-thousand-dollar profit on the sale. He moved all his belongings out to his cottage and settled in to enjoy the peace and quiet.

Harry loved spending all of his time with his son. When Harry, Jr., was 11 months old, he started to walk, and he was talking steadily soon thereafter.

Harry held a joint birthday party for them both. He was brimming with joy when his son turned one and he turned back to 33. Junior seemed to like the party, even though there were only the two of them present. Harry had brought out party hats and bought the boy a Cabbage Patch Kid for a present.

The years passed quickly, and with each that passed, Junior grew to be more and more like a little boy instead of a baby. By the time he was 5, Harry

had turned back to 29 and had lost all of the excess weight that he had put on. He felt trim and spent most of his time running through the wilderness with Junior or teaching him how to swim in the lake. Winters were a bit tiresome, since he was afraid to keep the boy out in the harsh wind and cold snow for long periods at a time, but that only made them appreciate the hot, dry summers all the more.

Harry Junior loved his dad in equal part. He never knew that living alone wasn't normal, although he was always excited when they would go for their monthly grocery trips into town.

Every second year, Harry would change the grocer that he used, since he didn't want any questions being asked.

By the time that Harry was 24 and Junior was 10, the townspeople started to think of them as brothers, rather than father and son. Even Harry sometimes thought of it that way.

Harry and Harry, Jr., both celebrated their seventeenth birthday on the same day. To mark the occasion, they double-dated two 16-year-old girls from town. Harry's date was a blonde girl who worked at the grocery store, and Harry, Jr.'s was a darkly tanned girl who worked part-time at the tennis club. They went to an evening showing of *The Night of the Living Dead* and then talked the girls into skinny-dipping off the end of a deserted pier.

The two boys shared a secret smile as they dropped their dates off later that night. They knew they couldn't date the girls for long without raising suspicions, but it was fun while it lasted. Both thought it was the best birthday they had ever spent, although Harry, Sr., sometimes had trouble remembering some of his older birthdays.

At 15, Harry started shaving only on alternate days, and soon gave it up altogether as his facial hair pulled back into his chin.

As Junior grew older, he started to pick up the responsibilities that his father could no longer handle. He was the one who now organized the shopping trips, holding his father's hand as they crossed the busy roads.

By the time that Harry, Sr., was 4, he was small enough for his son to cuddle with him. He had only vague recollections of his past, which were no more real than the flighty imaginings that any little boy has. Harry, Jr., loved the boy with all his heart and spent every minute with him, racing through the forest, wading in the lake, or whispering lullabies at night.

Harry, Sr., turned into a cranky baby, but by the time he was 11 months old, Junior hardly noticed. He carried his dad everywhere they went, although they didn't go quite as far as they had in the past, when Harry had been bigger. Junior put on quite a bit of weight from the lack of activity, and small worry wrinkles crept into his brow.

And soon, Harry Selkirk, Sr., disappeared.

Harry, Jr., was heartbroken, even though he had known that the day was coming. It was his 34th birthday, and all he could think about was his dead little father.

Junior spent a depressed month, drinking steadily. Finally, he managed to accept his father's death and built a small monument at the back of the cottage, near the woods.

He was lonely and looked up the little brunette he had started to date on his 17th birthday. They had kept in touch over the years, although nothing serious had ever developed. She still worked at the tennis club.

Harry asked her out more often, since he had nothing else to do with his time, and a couple of months later, they were married.

Harry, Jr., smiled the morning after their wedding night. He knew that his wife was now carrying his son.

Ω

SOMETHING FOR AMY

by Andrew Seawell

A package arrives for Amy. On the return address she reads that it's from Paul. With a sense of reluctance she begins to open it. What does he want now? Doesn't he know it's over?

She finds a note atop the wads of newspaper.

Dear Amy,

I've been going through my papers — all your love letters and all the pictures of us. I know what to do with those, but I found something here that I can't use. So I've sent it along to you via Vito who executed the contract for me. I would have sent it directly had such been possible. This will always be yours, so there is no point in its remaining with me.

Forever,
Paul

Puzzled, she digs deeper in the box and screams when she discovers his heart.

Ω

THE CHANGE

by Ramsey Campbell

As soon as he reached the flat Don started writing. Walking home, he'd shaped the chapter in his mind. What transformations does the werewolf undergo? he wrote. The new streetlamp by the bus-stop snapped alight as the October evening dimmed. Does he literally change into another creature, or is it simply a regression?

"How's it coming?" Margaret asked when she came in.

"Pretty well." It was, though she'd distracted him. He stared out at the bluish lamp and searched for the end of his sentence.

After dinner, during which his mind had been constructing paragraphs, he hurried back to his desk. The bluish light washed out the lines of ink; the rest of the page looked arctically indifferent, far too wide to fill. His prepared paragraphs grew feeble. When he closed the curtains and wrote a little, his sentences seemed dull. Tomorrow was Saturday. He'd begin early.

He had forgotten the queues at the bus-stop. He went unshaven to his desk, but already shoppers were chattering about the crowds they would avoid. They were less than three yards from him, and the glass seemed very thin. He was sure the noise grew worse each week. Still, he could ignore it, use the silences.

Aren't we all still primitive? he wrote. *Hasn't civilization* — Children whined, tugging at their mothers. *Hasn't civilization* — Now the women were shaking the children, cuffing them, shouting. *Hasn't bloody civilization* — A bus bore the queue away, but as many people missed the bus and began complaining loudly, repetitively.

"Yes, it's going all right," he told Margaret, and pretended to turn back to check a reference. He wasn't lying. Just a temporary block.

Hasn't civilization simply trapped and repressed our primitive instincts? he managed to stutter at last. *But the more strongly* Scarved crowds were massing outside, chanting football slogans. There's tribal behaviour for you. *But the more strongly* Youths stared in at him, shouting inanities. If only there was room in the bedroom for his desk, if only they had erected the bus-stop just a few houses away — He forced himself to keep his head down. *But the more strongly primitive instincts are repressed the more savage their occasional outburst will be, whether in mass murder or actual lycanthropy.* God, that was enough. Sunday would be better.

Sunday was full of children, playing itinerant games. He abandoned writing, and researched in library books while Margaret wrote her case reports. He was glad he'd taken time off to read the books. Now he had new insights, which would mean a stronger chapter.

Monday was hectic. The most complicated tax assessments were being calculated, now that all the information had arrived. Taxpayers phoned, demanding why they were waiting; the office rang incessantly. "Inland Revenue," Don and his colleagues kept saying. "Inland Revenue." Still, he managed to calculate three labyrinthine assessments.

He felt more confident on the way home. He was already on the third chapter, and his publisher had said that this book should be more commercial than his first. Perhaps it would pay for a house, then Margaret could give up social work and have her baby; perhaps he could even write full time. He strode home, determined to improve the book. Dissolving bars of gold floated in the deep blue sky, beyond the tower blocks.

He was surprised how well the opening chapters read. He substituted phrases here and there. The words grew pale as bluish light invaded his desk-lamp's. When the text gave out, his mind went on. His nib scratched faintly. At the end of the second paragraph he gazed out, frowning.

The street had the unnatural stillness of a snowscape. Street and houses stretched away in both directions, gleaming faintly blue. The cross-street on his right was lit similarly; the corner house had no shadow. The pavement seemed oppressively close with no garden intervening. Everything looked unreal, glary with lightning.

He was so aware of the silence now that it distracted him. He must get an idea moving before the silence gave way, before someone came to stare. Write, for God's sake write. Repression, regression, lycanthropy. It sounded like a ditty in his mind.

Animal traits of primitive man. Distrust of the unfamiliar produces a savage response. He scribbled, but there seemed to be no continuity; his thoughts were flowing faster than his ink. Someone crossed at the intersection, walking oddly. He glared at the shadowless corner, but it was deserted. At the edge of his vision the figure had looked as odd as the light. He scribbled, crossing out and muttering to deafen himself to the silence. As he wrote the end of a paragraph, a face peered at him, inches from his. Margaret had tiptoed up to smile. He crumpled the book as he slammed it shut, but managed to smile as she came in.

Later he thought an idea was stirring, a paragraph assembling. Margaret began to tell him about her latest case.

"Right, yes, all right," he muttered and sat at the window, his back to her. The blank page blotted thought from his mind. The bluish light tainted the page and the desk, like a sour indefinable taste.

The light bothered him. It changed his view of the quiet street which he'd used to enjoy while working. This new staged street was unpleasantly compelling. Passers-by looked discoloured, almost artificial. If he drew the curtains, footsteps conjured up caricatures which strolled across his mind. If he sat at the dining-table he could still hear any footsteps, and was nearer Margaret, the rustling of her case reports, her laughter as she read a book.

His head was beginning to feel like the approach of a storm; he wasn't sure how long it had felt that way. The first sign of violence was almost a relief. It was Thursday night, and he was straining at a constipated paragraph. When someone arrived at the bus-stop, Don forced himself not to look. He gazed at the blot which had gathered at the end of his last word, where he'd rested his pen. The blot had started to look like an obstacle he would never be able to pass. The bluish light appeared to be making it grow, and there was another blot on the edge of his vision — another man at the bus-stop. If he looked he would never be able to write, he knew. At last he glanced up, to get it over with, and then he stared. Something was wrong.

They looked almost like two strangers at a bus-stop, their backs to each other. One shrugged his shoulders loosely, as though he was feeling the cold; the other stretched, baring huge calloused hands. Their faces were neutral as masks. All at once Don saw that was just a pretence. Each man was waiting for the other to make a move. They were wary as animals in a cage.

Now he could see how whenever one shifted the other turned towards him, almost imperceptibly. The light had changed their faces into plastic, bluish plastic masks that might at any moment slip awry. Suddenly Don's mouth tasted sour, for he'd realized that the men were turning their backs on the roadway; before they came face to face, they would see him. He was protected by the window, and anyway he could retreat to Margaret. But the sound of her rustling pages seemed very far away. Now the masks were almost facing him, and a roar was growing — the sound of a bus. He managed to gulp back a sigh of relief before Margaret could notice that anything was wrong. How could he explain to her when he didn't understand it himself?

When the men had boarded the bus, making way stiffly for each other, he closed the curtains hastily. His fingers were trembling, and he had to go into the kitchen to splash cold water on his face. Trying to appear nonchalant as he passed Margaret, he felt as false as the masks in the street.

A face came towards the window, grinning. It was discoloured, shiny, plastic; its eyes shone, unnaturally blue. As it reached the window it cracked like an egg from forehead to chin, and its contents leapt at him, smashing the glass and his dream. Beside him Margaret was sound asleep. He lay in his own dark and wondered what was true about the dream.

The next night he pretended to write, and watched. His suspicion was absurd, but fascinating. As he gazed unblinking at the people by the bus-stop they looked increasingly deformed; their heads were out of proportion, or their faces lopsided; their dangling hands looked swollen and clumsy. Christ, nobody was perfect; the clinical light simply emphasized imperfections, or his eyes were tired. Yet the people looked self-conscious, pretending to be normal. That light would make anyone feel awkward. He would be glad of Saturday and daylight.

He'd forgotten the crowds again. Once they would have set him scribbling his impressions in his notebook; now their mannerisms looked studied and ugly, their behaviour uncivilized. The women were mannequins, in hideous taste: hives of artificially senile hair squatted on their heads, their eyes looked enlarged with blue paint. The men were louder and more brutal, hardly bothering to pretend at all.

Margaret returned, laden with shopping. "I saw your book in the supermarket. I improved their display."

"Good, fine," he snarled, and tried to reconstruct the sentence she had ruined. He was gripping his pen so hard it almost cracked.

On Sunday afternoon he managed a page, as late sunlight turned the street amber. In one case, he wrote, a man interested in transmogrification took LSD and "became" a tiger, even to seeing a tiger in the mirror. *Doesn't this show how fragile human personality is?* Too many bloody rhetorical questions in this book. *Very little pressure is needed to break the shell of civilization, of all that we call human* — five minutes more of that bloody radio upstairs was about all it would take. There was no silence anywhere, except the strained unnerving quiet of the street at night.

Next week Margaret was on call. After being surrounded by the office phones all day, he was even more on edge for the shrilling of the phone. Yet when she was called out he was surprised to find that he felt relieved. The flat was genuinely silent, for the people overhead were out too. Though he was tired from persuading irate callers that they owed tax, he uncapped his pen and sat at the window.

Why is the full moon important to lycanthropy? Does moonlight relate to a racial memory, a primitive fear? Its connotations might stir up the primitive elements of the personality, most violently where they were most repressed, or possibly where they were closest to the surface. Come to think, it must be rather like the light outside his window.

There was his suspicion again, and yet he had no evidence. He'd seen how the light caricatured people, and perhaps its spotlighting made them uneasy. But how could a streetlight make anyone more savage — for example, the gang of youths he could hear approaching loudly? It was absurd. Nevertheless his palms were growing slick with apprehension, and he could hardly keep hold of his pen.

When they came abreast of the window they halted and began to jeer at him, at his pose behind the desk. Teeth gleamed metallically in the discoloured faces, their eyes glittered like glass. For a moment he was helpless with panic, then he realized that the glass protected him. He held that thought steady, though his head was thumping. Let them try to break through, he'd rip their throats out on the glass, drag their faces over the splinters. He sat grinning at the plastic puppets while they jeered and gestured jerkily. At last they dawdled away, shouting threats.

He sat coated with the light, and felt rather sick. He seemed unable to clear his mind of a jumble of images: glass, flesh, blood, screams. He got up to find a book, any distraction at all, and then he saw his bluish shadow. Its long hands dangled, its distorted head poked forward. As he stooped to peer closer he felt as if it was dragging him down, stretching his hands down to meet its own. All at once he darted to the light-switch. He clawed the curtains shut and left the light burning, then he went into the bedroom and sat for a long time on the bed. He held his face as though it was a mask that was slipping.

On Thursday the bus home was delayed by a car crash. While the other passengers stared at blood and deformed metal, Don was uneasily watching the night seep across the sky. When he reached home the house looked worse than he'd feared: thin, cardboardy, bricks blackened by the light — not much of a refuge at all.

He was overworked, that was why he felt nervous. He must find time to relax. He'd be all right once he was inside with the curtains drawn, away from the dead light that seemed to have soaked into everything, even his fingers as they fumbled with the key. He glanced up to see who was watching him from the upstairs flat, then he looked away hastily. Maybe someone up there was really as deformed as that; he never met the tenants, they had a separate entrance. No, surely the figure must have looked like that because of a flaw in the glass.

In his flat he listened to the footsteps overhead, and couldn't tell if anything was wrong with them. Eventually he cooked the dinner Margaret had left him when she was called away. He tried to write, but the fragility of the silence made him too nervous. When he held his breath, he could hear the jungle of sound beyond the curtains: snarls of cars, the low thunder of planes, shouts, things falling, shrieks of metal, cries. The bluish flat stood emptily behind him.

The last singers were spilling out of pubs. Surely Margaret would be home soon. Wasn't that Margaret now? No, the hurrying footsteps were too uneven and too numerous: a man and a woman. He could hear the man shouting incoherently, almost wordlessly. Now the woman was running, and the man was stumbling heavily after her. When he caught her outside the window she began to scream.

Don squirmed in his chair. She was screaming abuse, not with fear. He could stand it, surely it wouldn't last long, her screeching voice that seemed to be in the room with him, scraping his nerves. All at once a body thumped the window; the frame shook. They were fighting, snarling. Christ! He struggled to his feet and forced himself to reach towards the curtains.

Then he saw the shadows, and barely managed not to cry out himself. Though the curtains blurred them, they were all too clear to him. As they clawed at each other, he was sure their arms were lengthening. Surely their heads were swelling like balloons and changing shape; perhaps that was why they sounded as though they never could have formed words. The window juddered and he flinched back, terrified they might sense him beyond the glass. For a moment he saw their mouths lunging at each other's faces, tearing.

All at once there was silence. Footsteps stumbled away, he couldn't tell whose. It took him a long time to part the curtains, and much longer to open the front door. But the street was deserted, and he might have doubted everything he'd seen but for a smear of blood on the window. He ran for tissues and wiped it away, shuddering. The lamp stood behind him, bright and ruthless; its dead eye gazed from the pane. He was surrounded. He could only take refuge in bed and try to keep his eyes closed.

The next day he rang the Engineering Department (Mechanical & Lighting) from the office, and told them where he lived. "What exactly have you put in those lights?"

The girl was probably just a clerk. "No, they're not mercury vapour," he said. "You might think they were, but not if you had to live with them, I can tell you. Will you connect me with someone who knows?"

Perhaps she felt insulted, or perhaps his tone disturbed her. "Never mind why I want to know. You don't want me to know, do you? Well, I know there's something else in them, let me tell you, and I'll be in touch with someone who can do something about it."

As he slammed the receiver down, he saw that his colleagues were staring at him. What was wrong with them? Had the politeness which the job demanded possessed them completely? Were they scared of a bit of honest rage?

On the way home he wandered until he found a derelict area, though the start of winter time had made him more nervous. Already the sky was black, an hour earlier than yesterday, and he was dismayed to find he dreaded going home. Outside his flat the lamp stood waiting, in a street that looked alien as the moon. Nobody was in sight. He unlocked the front door, then he lifted the brick he was carrying and hurled it at the lamp. As the bulb shattered, he closed the door quickly. He spent the evening pretending to write, and stared out at the dark.

Saturday brought back the crowds. Their faces were pink putty, all too malleable. He cursed himself for wasting last night's dark. If he went to the library for quiet he would have walked two miles for nothing: there would be crowds there too. If only he could afford to move! But it was only the cheap rent here that was allowing him and Margaret to save.

She emerged from the mass of putty faces and dumped shopping on the table. "Isn't it going well?"

"What do you mean, isn't it going well? It won't go better for questions like that, will it? Yes, of course it's going well!" There was no point in telling her the truth; he had enough to bear without her anxiety. That evening he wrote a few paragraphs, but they were cumbersome and clumsy.

On Sunday he tried to relax, but whenever Margaret spoke he felt there was an idea at the edge of his mind, waiting to be glimpsed and written. "Yes, later, later," he muttered, trying vainly to recapture the idea. That night she turned restlessly in bed for hours. He lay beside her and wondered uneasily what had gone wrong with the dark.

His lack of sleep nagged him on Monday. His skull felt tight and fragile. Whenever he tried to add up a column of figures a telephone rang, his colleagues laughed inanely, a fragment of conversation came into focus. People wandered from desk to desk. His surroundings were constantly restless, distracting.

One of his taxpayers called and refused to believe he owed four hundred pounds. Don sensed how the man's hands were clenching, seeking a victim, reaching for him. There was no need to panic, not with the length of the telephone cable between them. He couldn't be bothered to conceal his feelings. "You owe the money. There's nothing I can do."

"You bastards," the man was screaming, "you f—" as Don put down the receiver.

Some of his colleagues were staring at him. Maybe they could have done better, except that they probably wouldn't even have realized they were threatened. Did they honestly believe that words and printed forms were answers to the violence? Couldn't they see how false it all was? Only his triumph over the streetlamp helped him through the day.

He walked most of the way home, enjoying the darkness where lamps were smashed. As he neared his street the bluish light closed in. It didn't matter, it couldn't reach his home now. When he began to run, anxious to take refuge, his footsteps sounded flat and false as the light. He turned the corner into his street. Outside his flat the lamp was lit.

It craned its bony concrete neck, a tall thin ghost, its face blazing. It had defeated him. However many times he destroyed it, it would return. He locked himself in and grabbed blindly for the light-switch.

After dinner he sat at his desk and read his chapters, in case Margaret suspected he had failed. The words on the bluish pages seemed meaningless; even his handwriting looked unfamiliar. His hot eyes felt unfamiliar too.

And now it was Margaret's noises. They sounded forced, unnervingly artificial, sound effects. When he frowned at her she muted them, which only made them more infuriating. Her eyes were red, but he couldn't help it if she was distressed while he felt as he did, besieged deep in himself. "I'm going to bed," she said eventually, like a rebuke. When he couldn't bear sitting alone any longer, she was still awake. He lay with his back to her in order to discourage conversation, which would distract him. Something was certainly wrong with the dark.

In the morning, when she'd gone to work, he saw what he must do. Since he had no chance of writing at weekends or in the evenings, he must give up his daytime job, which was false anyway. His book was more important, it would say things that needed saying — they would be clear when the time came to write them. In the shaving mirror his grin looked weaker than he felt.

He grinned more widely as he phoned to report himself sick. That falseness was enjoyable. He sat grinning at his desk, waiting for words. But he couldn't reach back to the self who had written the chapters; however deep in his mind he groped, there was nothing but a dialogue. Isn't it going well? No, it isn't going well. No, it isn't, no, it isn't, no, it isn't going well. Repression, regression, lycanthropy. Putty faces bobbed past the window. Now here was the bluish light, moulding them into caricatures or worse. Repression, regression, lycanthropy.

"You're home early," Margaret said. He stared at her, probing for the implication, until she looked away.

After dinner she watched television in the bedroom, with the sound turned to a whisper. He followed her, to place more distance between himself and the tinged curtains. As soon as he switched off the light, the living-room was a dead bluish box. When he clawed at the switch, the bluish tinge seemed to have invaded the light of the room.

"You've left the light on."

"Leave it on!" He couldn't tell her why. He was trapped in himself, and his shell felt brittle. In a way it was a relief to be cut off from her that way; at least he needn't struggle to explain. She stared at the screen, she swallowed aspirin, she glanced at him and flinched from his indifferent gaze. Shrunken figures jerked about as though they were trying to escape the box of the television, and they felt as real as he did. After a while Margaret slipped into bed and hid her face. He supposed she was crying.

He lay beside her. Voices crowded his mind, shouting. Repression, regression, lycanthropy. Margaret's hand crept around his waist, but he couldn't bear to be touched; he shook her off. Perhaps she was asleep. Around him the room was faintly luminous. He gazed at it suspiciously until his eyelids drooped.

When he woke, he seemed hardly to have slept. Perhaps the revelation had woken him, for he knew at last what was wrong with the dark. It had developed a faint bluish tinge. How could the light penetrate the closed door? Was it reaching beneath the door for him? Or had the colour settled on his eyeballs, seeped into them?

It hadn't trapped him yet. He sneaked into his clothes. Margaret was a vague draped huddle, dimly bluish. He tiptoed to the front door and let himself out, then he began to run.

At the tower blocks he slowed. Concrete, honeycombed with curtained rectangles, massed above him. Orange sodium mushrooms glared along the paths, blackening the grass. The light outside his flat was worse than that; it was worse than moonlight, because it infected everyone, not just the few. That was why he'd felt so strange lately. It had been transforming him.

He must go back for Margaret. They must leave now, this minute. Tomorrow they'd find somewhere else to live, draw on their savings; they could come back in daylight for their possessions. He must go back, he'd left her alone with the light. He ran, closing his eyes against the light as far as he could.

As he reached the street he heard someone padding towards him — padding like an animal. He dodged into an alley almost opposite the flat, but the padding turned aside somewhere. He grinned at the dark; he could outwit the light now that he knew its secret. But as soon as he emerged into the street he sensed that he was being watched.

He saw the face almost at once. It was staring at him between curtains, beside a reflection of the lamp. The face was a luminous dead mask, full of the light. He could see the animal staring out through the eyes. The mask was inside his flat, staring out at him.

He made himself go forward, or perhaps the light was forcing him. Certainly it had won. His head felt cold and hollow, cut off from his trudging. The eyes widened in the mask; the creature was ready to fly at him. The mask writhed, changing.

Suddenly he caught sight of his shadow. The light was urging it towards the window. Its claws were dangling, its head swelled forward eagerly, and this time there was nothing familiar to hold him back, no light he could switch on to change the dead street and the shadow. There was only the enemy in his home. He was the shadow, one hand dangling near the gutter. He snatched up the brick and smashing the window, struggled in through the splintering frame.

The creature backed away, into a corner. For a moment it seemed to be beaten. But when he leapt, hurling the curtains aside, it fought him with its claws. He struggled with it, breaking it, biting, tearing. At last it was still. He staggered blindly into the bedroom, mopping blood from his eyes with the rags of his sleeve.

He switched on the light, but couldn't

tell what colour it was. He felt like a hollow shell. When at last he noticed that the bed was empty, it took him a very long time to force himself to look in the living-room. As he looked, he became less and less sure of what he was seeing. As to who was seeing it, he had no idea at all. Ω

THE FINAL DEATH OF THE COMEBACK KING

by Bruce Bethke

We melted into the crowd along Pennsylvania Avenue and watched the black-draped caisson as it rolled slowly past. The horse's black plumes sagged in the light summer rain; their hooves clip-clopped on the wet pavement in soft syncopation to the slow throb of the muffled drums.

"It's the end of an era," said Weaver, of the *Post,* on my left.

"We can only hope," said Vaccaro, of the *Times,* on my right.

The Marines marched past in dark, majestic precision.

Weaver looked down at his wet brown shoes, and softly shook his head. "I still have trouble believing the man's really gone. I mean, he made a *career* out of dramatic comebacks. Washed up as an actor, he turned to politics."

"Declared politically dead after the '68 election," Vaccaro added, "he came back stronger than ever in '76."

Weaver looked up, and brushed back a vagrant strand of wet hair that had fallen in his face. "Elected president, he survived two impossible assassination attempts. I can accept that Helsing missed at point-blank range. It must be hard to aim with Secret Service agents tackling you."

"But to survive the Stinger that took out Air Force One and killed the entire cabinet..." Vaccaro could only shake his head.

We stood quietly awhile longer, watching the funeral cortege plod along the wet, dreary street, making its slow way to the final resting place.

"What do you think?" Weaver asked, turning to me. "Any way he can come back from *this?*"

"There's one way to make sure," I said.

Late that evening, after the crowds and the TV cameras had gone away, we broke into the Capitol. The President's casket stood on a flag-draped catafalque beneath the rotunda. We caught him just as he was releasing the internal latches.

He put up quite a struggle when we drove the wooden stake through his heart. Ω

IMPROBABLE BESTIARY: THE BLOB

Oh, it fell from the sky on a night in July;
Its arrival was quite surreptitious.
It began as a speck of mysterious dreck,
But it proved itself highly ambitious.
For it turned into goo which resembled a brew
Made of gelatin, glue, and a leftover stew —
And it grew and it grew and it grew and it *grew*
Till it swallowed six cows and a farmer or two,
Smacked its lips, and exclaimed, *"How delicious!"*

Oh, it came up the street seeking something to eat
But the townspeople saw the Blob coming
And they bolted the doors and plugged up all the floors;
So it shrugged, and came in through the plumbing.
All the people it met were extremely upset
To be eaten like so many pickles.
Lots of children were screaming (and likewise adults)
When along came the scientist Ludwig von Schultz.
"I can kill it," he said, "and I promise results!"
Then he blasted the Blob with a few billion volts
But the Blob just replied: "Hey, that *tickles!*"

Oh, we stared in surprise while it increased in size
Till the Blob got so big it could dwarf us.
"We're doomed!" someone cried. "Now the Blob's a mile wide,
And besides that . . . it's all *polymorphous!"*
There were shouts of disorder and "Head for the border
Before that big Blob tries to flatten us!
It's a gluttonous, glutinous, thoroughly mutinous
Blob that's completely *gelatinous!"*

Oh, the Blob shook like Jell-O, turned orange and yellow,
And polka-dot plaid polychromic.
Then it headed northeast, chomping human and beast,
While it ate its way up the Potomac.
It digested its fill up on Capitol Hill;
There was clearly no way to appease it.
Then a kid in the crowd shouted out very loud:
"We can stop the Blob now if we *freeze it!"*

Well, we ended the slaughter with sprays of ice water;
The Blob never knew we'd defeat it.
Now we keep it ice-cold in a gelatin mold,
And as soon as it's frozen . . . we'll *eat it!*
Everyone gets a slice of the Blob served on ice
(Say, it's not too much work for the chef, is it?)
And with whipped cream for topping, the Blob is so whopping
It's as big as the federal deficit.

— F. Gwynplaine MacIntyre

IT GROWS ON YOU

by Stephen King

New England autumn and the thin soil now shows in patches through the ragweed and goldenrod, waiting for snow still four weeks distant, leaves clogged in culverts. The sky has gone a perpetual waiting gray and corn stalks stand in leaning rows. Pumpkins, sagging inward now with softrot, are piled against crepuscular sheds. There is no heat and no cold, only pallid air which is never still, beating through the bare fields and snuffling into junked cars up on blocks in back yards.

The Newall house on the Stackpole Road overlooks Southwest Bend; vacant and brown and washed by the weather, the front lawn a mass of dried hummocks which the frost will soon heave into even more grotesque postures. Thin smoke rises from the store at the Bend below. On the old bandstand across the road two small children roll a red firetruck between them. Their faces are tired and washed out. Their hands actually seem to cut the air as they roll the truck between them, and their noses run.

In the store Harley McKissick is presiding, corpulent and red-faced, while John Bowen and John Matterly sit by the stove with their feet up. Paul Corliss is leaning against the counter. The store has a smell that is ancient, a smell of salami and flypaper and coffee and tobacco, sweat, brown Coca Cola, pepper, cloves, Bay Rum. Old announcements of town meetings dot the walls: a flyspecked poster advertising a beanhole bean supper held in 1962 still leans in the window, perpetually curled and browned by nine July suns. At the back of the store there is a huge glass freezer that came out of New York in 1923, a meat grinder, and a Kingston scale with a large dial.

The old men watch the children, speaking in low desultory tones. John Matterly has been talking about the town dump, which stinks in the summertime. No one is really interested because it is not summer, it is autumn, and the huge range-oil stove is throwing off a stuporous glow of heat. The Winston thermometer behind the counter says 82. John Matterley's forehead has a huge dent just to the right of his left temple where he struck his head in a car accident in the year 1953. Small children often ask to touch it. He has won a great deal of money from summer people who don't believe the dent will hold the contents of a medium-sized water tumbler.

"Paulson," Harley McKissick says quietly.

An old Chevrolet has pulled slowly in behind John Bowen's pickup. On the side is a cardboard sign held with heavy masking tape which reads GARY PAULSON CHAIRS CANED ANTIQUES 353-8792. Gary Paulson gets out slowly, an old man in faded green pants, holding to the doorframe until he is properly supported. The cane has a white bicycle handgrip for traction at its tip. It makes small circles in the lifeless dust as he begins toward the door.

The children on the bandstand look up at him fearfully, then at the leaning, crepitating bulk of the Newall house on the hill. Then they go back to their truck.

Joe Newall came to Harlow in 1904

and owned in Harlow until his death in 1929, but his fortune was made across the river in Gates Falls. He was a scrawny man with an angry, hectic face and eyes with yellow corneas. He bought a great parcel of land in south Harlow, Phil Burdeau's land, from The First Bank in Lewiston, who held the mortgage. The land was very cheap, and Phil Burdeau, who had been well-liked in town, slunk away to Kittery where he did badly as a mechanic who specialized in Ford A's and T's. The land lay silent for twelve years while Joe Newall lived in a rented house in Gates Falls and saw to the making of his fortune. He became foreman of the carding room of the Gates Mill in 1908, and the women worked under his supervision like frightened darkies. In 1914 he wived Cora Leonard, niece of Carl Stowe. The marriage had great merit because Carl Stowe was co-founder and now, since the death of Gabe Gates (old, stupid, senile, wracked with both Parkinson's Disease and uremic poisoning, Carl Stowe's business partner died in bed at the age of seventy-nine, still the town's head selectman and overseer of the poor), sole owner of the mill. Cora did not have merit. She was a grain-bag of a woman, moonlike and silent. Her face was clay. She sweated huge patches around the armholes of her dresses even in February. If thoughts or fantasies grew in the dark soil of her brain she did not say.

The house which Joe Newall built for his wife in Harlow was completed in 1916. It was painted white and enclosed twelve rooms. It sprouted from many strange angles. Joe Newall was not popular in Harlow because he made his money out of town (although very few made money in Harlow — by 1916 the town was moribund) and because his house was built without town labor. Shortly before the house was roofed an obscene drawing accompanied by a one-syllable Anglo-Saxon word was scrawled on the fanlighted front-door in soft yellow chalk.

By 1920 Joe Newall was a rich man and the Gates Mill was a rich enterprise, stuffed with the profits of a world war. He began to build an unnecessary wing to his house, which most agreed was ugly beyond words already. The wing towered one story above the main house and looked blindly down a hill covered with straggling pines. The wing was in the nature of a celebration; Cora Leonard Newall had conceived after four years of wedded bliss during which she existed in the collective mind of the town as a specter who could be seen only at a distance as she crossed her dooryard or occasionally picking wildflowers — crocuses, wild roses, Queen Anne's lace, paintbrush — in the field beyond the outbuildings. Small boys giggled at her and made crude jokes, but walked hand in hand past the house at twilight. She did her marketing at the Kitty Korner Store in Gates Center every Thursday.

In January of 1921 Cora Leonard Newall gave birth to a mewling monstrosity with no arms which died in the Newall bedchamber six hours after mindless contraction had pushed it into the light. Joe Newall added a cupola to the wing in 1922. A lightning rod jutted starkly against the sky. He also bought out of town and would have nothing to do with Irv McKissick's store or with the Harlow Methodist Church. The deformed infant which had slid from Cora Leonard Newall's womb was buried in the Newall plot in Gates Falls. The inscription on the tiny headstone read SARAH TAMSON NEWALL JANUARY 14, 1921 "GOING BEFORE."

They talked in the store, about Joe Newall and Joe Newall's wife and Joe Newall's house, as Irv's kid Harley, wrapped in a white butcher's apron, cut meat and wrapped orders. Mostly it was the house of which they spoke; it was considered to be an ugly, brazen affront. "But it grows on you," John Bowen often said in those days. There was no

answer for this. It was a patent fact.

In 1924 Cora Leonard Newall fell down the stairs between the cupola and the new wing, breaking both her neck and her back. A rumor went through town (started, perhaps, by the Methodist Ladies' Aid) that she had been naked at the time. She was interred next to her daughter.

Joe Newall, who, most people now agreed, contained a touch of the kike, continued to make money hand over hand. He built two sheds and a barn, all of which jutted off from the new wing. The barn was completed in 1927 and Joe bought sixteen cows from a fellow in Mechanic Falls. He also bought a shiny new milking machine that looked like an octopus and hired a halfwit from Gates Falls to care for the animals. The cows died that summer of what was rumored to be anthrax. The half-wit, clad in dung-splattered bib overalls from the Sears and Roebuck mail-order catalogue, leaned against the Newall rural delivery box and wept monotonously all that yellow August day. The town health officer, who came to investigate, was met at the edge of the dooryard by Joe Newall and the vet from Gates Falls. The vet had a sworn affidavit which testified that the cows had died of non-infectious meningitis.

"I want to see the cows," the health officer said.

"No," said Joe Newall.

"I can get a court order."

"Get it."

The health officer drove away and Joe and the vet watched him go while the half-wit clutched the mailbox and wept at the sky.

The health officer, Clem Upshaw from Bowie Hill, would have dropped the matter at the sight of the affidavit, but he had been elected with the help of his good friend Irv McKissick, who got him on the ballot unopposed, and Irv wanted to make a point with Joe Newall — that private property is still stitched to the town, that Harlow protected its own. So Clem Upshaw got the order.

While he was getting it a large van had driven up to the Newall barn. When Clem Upshaw returned with his order only one cow remained, stiffening in its stall, gazing up at Clem with dull black eyes covered with hay chaff. The cow's body had been pulled into a painful, bulging rictus. Tiny fleas still jumped on its hide. Clem determined that the cow died of non-infectious meningitis and went away. The van returned once more for the last cow.

In 1928 Joe Newall began another wing. That was when it was decided that Joe was crazy, smart but crazy. Benny Wing claimed that Joe had gouged out the eyes of his deformed daughter, his wife, and his cows. Benny claimed that Joe kept them in a jar on the kitchen table. Benny was a great reader of the horror pulps, the ones that showed naked ladies being carried off by giant ants with their eyes swaying at the ends of long, hairy stalks, and his story about Joe Newall was obviously a lie. As a result, the story gained quite a following in town. Some claimed that Joe kept less mentionable things in the jar.

The second wing was finished in August of 1929 and two nights later a fast-moving jalopy with great sodium circles for eyes screamed juddering into Joe Newall's driveway and a freshly killed chicken was thrown at the new wing. The bird splattered above one of the windows, throwing a fan of blood across the panes in a pattern almost like a Chinese ideogram.

In September of 1929 a fire swept the carding room of the Gates Mill, spread to the sorting room, and caused $500,000 worth of damage. In October the stock market crashed. In November, with the smell of burnt leaves hanging over the town like an incantation, Joe Newall hanged himself in one of the unfurnished bedrooms of the newest wing. The smell of sap in the fresh wood was still strong. He was found by Cleve Torbutt, the assistant manager of the Gates Mill, Joe's partner (or so it was rumored) in a great many Wall Street ventures that were now not worth the puke of a tubercular she-bitch. The body was cut down by the county coroner, who was from Lewiston.

Joe was buried with his wife and child on December 1 of that year. It was a hard, brilliant day and the only person from Harlow to attend the services was Alvin Coy, who drove the Hay & Peabody funeral hack. Alvin reported that one of the spectators was a young, shapely woman who wore a raccoon coat with a black fur collar. Sitting in McKissick's store and eating a pickle, Alvin would smile mordantly and tell his cronies that she was a jazz baby if he ever seen one. She bore not the slightest resemblance to Cora Leonard Newall's side of the family; and she did not close her eyes during the prayer.

Gary Paulson enters the store with exquisite slowness, closing the door carefully behind him.

"Afternoon, " Harley McKissick says neutrally.

"Heard you won a turkey at the Grange last night," John Bowen says. He has produced a hoary corncob pipe and begins to tamp Prince Albert into the bowl with a slow and dreamy finger.

"Yuh," Gary says. He is eighty-four and can remember when Harlow was livelier than it is now. He lost two sons in the second war, which was a hard thing. A third, who was a no-good, died in a car accident on the Maine Turnpike near Clinton in 1955. Gary sometimes drools and his lips make odd smacking noises when he speaks.

"Coffee?" Harley asks.

"Guess not."

John Matterly pulls back his feet considerably so the old man can pass by him and lower himself into the chair in the corner. He smacks his lips and folds his hands, which are lumpy with arthri-

tis, over the head of his cane. He looks tired and haggard.

"It is going to rain," he says finally. "I am aching like a Spanish bastard."

"It's a bad fall," Paul Corliss says.

There is silence. The heat from the stove fills the store and the bones of the old men, who have seen their children go away to more profitable places. The store does no business to speak of now, except for the summer tourists who think the old men sitting around in their thermal undershirts during July are quaint, and those who have always traded here. These are fewer now, and most of them have the smell of the grave already on them. John Bowen has always claimed that new people are going to come probably with trailers, to escape Portland and Lewiston, but they never have.

"Who is building the new wing on that Christly Newall house?" Gary asks finally.

They look around at him. For a moment the kitchen match John Bowen has just scratched hangs mystically over his pipe, burning down the wood, turning it black . . . The burnt sulphur node at the end curls up. Then he dips it into the bowl and puffs.

"New wing?" Harley asks.

"Yuh."

A slow raft of Prince Albert drifts up and over the stove. John Matterly runs a slow hand over the salt-and-pepper stubble on his chin.

"No one that I know of," Harley says.

"They ain't had a buyer on that place since 1951," Bowen says. *They* is, of course, Gates Mills & Weaving, Inc., who succeeded to the title when Joe Newall ended his life. This, as they all knew, was Legal Stuff. The Mill's agent was Walker Bros., Inc., a realty agency located in Gates Falls. They have tried to agent a great many properties in Harlow during the years of the town's decline, and have actually succeeded in a few places, as in the case of that crazy wop from Pennsylvania who was going to raise racing horses on the old Wing farm (the wop, who smiled a lot and ran gallons of Vitalis through his black hair, went through bankruptcy a year later and departed for an unknown destination); so the Walker brothers are generally referred to in town as Those Goddamn Sheenies From Gates. No one has offered to buy the house since the Walker Bros. sign first went up in June of 1930, following the disposition of Joe Newall's earthly affairs. There have been a few leases with option to buy, but that is the long and tall of it.

"The last ones was those people from Massachusetts," John Bowen says. "They was a nice couple. Gonna paint the barn red and have cows, he was. You remember that, Harley?"

"Sure."

"They bought up in Auburn," John Bowen says uneasily. "Ain't that right?"

"Yuh," Gary Paulson says, "Moved, though."

"No one new that I know of," Harley says with finality.

"There is a new wing going up," Gary says. "I saw it coming down the river road. Most of the frame already. Prob'ly forty foot long and twenty wide. Never noticed it before. Nice pine. Points off from that first one that Newall built in '20."

"You're thinking of another house," Harley says uneasily.

"Guess not," Gary says softly, calmly.

In that case, there is nothing left to say. No one rushes outside to crane up at the Newall house. They suspect it may be a matter of some importance, and thus nothing to hurry over.

More time passes; Harley McKissick has, at times, reflected that if time were pulp-wood, they would all be rich. Paul Corliss goes to the old water-cooled soft-drink cooler and gets an Orange Crush. He gives his twelve cents to Harley, who rings it up. They are ready to put the subject of the Newall house in the active file and move on.

John Matterly sighs, crosses his legs laboriously, and says to Gary: "When are they having services for Dana Roy?"

"Tomorrow, in Gorham. That's where his wife is." Dana Roy's wife died in childbirth in 1948; Dana, who was an electrician for the Gates Mill until 1930 and then for the U.S. Gypsum in Freecastle until his retirement in 1956, died of intestinal cancer three days before. He had lived in Harlow all his life, and had only been out of Maine three times: once to visit an aunt in Indiana at the age of ten, once to see the Boston Red Sox play at Fenway Park at the age of twenty-five, once to attend an electricians' convention in Portsmouth, New Hampshire at the age of forty-seven ("Damn waste of time — nothing but drinkin and women, and none of the women worth a tinker's damn."). He has, of course, been these men's crony. In his passing they feel an admixture of fear, triumph, and sorrow.

"They took out four feet of his underpinnin," Gary says with flat finality. "Didn't do no good. It had him by the balls."

"He knew Joe Newall," John Matterly says. "Worked nine years for him, putting in electricity when the mill was switchin over. You 'member that, Harley?"

"Yup." All the men here, with the exception of Harley, have worked at the Gates Mill or Gypsum or Bates Woollens at some time during their lives. Most of them are now carefully searching for anecdotes concerning one man or the other. But when John Bowen finally speaks, he says a rather startling thing:

"I always had a suspicion it was Dana got those other boys to throw that chicken that time."

They look at him gravely.

"In '29," John elaborates.

"Yuh," Gary says. He shifts his seat, breaks wind, and readjusts his cane beside his chair. "Dana never cared so much for Joe."

"No one in Harlow did," John Bowen said. Silence again. The children on the bandstand have left and still the depthless afternoon continues on and on, the light that of a Wyeth painting, still and yet full of idiot meaning. The ground has given up its meager yield and waits for the snow.

Gary would like to tell them of the sick-room at the Central Maine General Hospital where Dana Roy lay dying, smelling yellow, black snot caked around his nose, would like to tell them of the cool blue tiles and the nurses with their hair drawn back in buns and hidden under nets, not knowing that 1920 was a real year, that old men's bones cry out in their bodies. He felt that he would like to sermonize on the evil that lay over them and beyond them, multiplying. Most of all he would like to tell them that Dana Roy sounded as if he were breathing through straw, and that he looked as if he were rotting already. Gary Paulson had pulled many rocks whole from the earth; the physical was his only frame of reference. Thus defeated, he said nothing.

"No sir, no one liked old Joe much," John Bowen repeats. His lips suddenly part, showing baby-smooth gums in a fleshless cackle. "But by God, he grew on you."

Nineteen days later, a week before the first snow comes to cover the useless earth, Gary Paulson dies suddenly in his sleep of a brain hemorrhage precipitated by a surprisingly sexual dream. On August 14, 1922, while driving by the Newall house in his farm truck, Gary Paulson, young and full of seminal sap (at that time liberally distributed between three young girls from the south Harlow area), happened to observe Cora Leonard Newall bending into the mailbox by the road to get the daily paper. A hot and vagrant gust of wind happened by, blowing back her skirt and revealing a perfectly naked, perfectly flawless female backside. It is an incident that he has never mentioned, no matter how strong the temptation. He has hoarded it. And it is of this incident that he is dreaming, penis perfectly erect at the age of eighty-three (perfectly erect for the first and only time in the last eleven years), when a small blood vessel in his cerebellum ruptures, forming a clot which kills him quietly, considerately sparing him a month or a year of paralysis, the flexible tubes in the arms, the catheter, the noiseless nurses with their hair in buns and their feet encased in ghostly crepe shoes. He dies calmly in his sleep, penis wilting, dream fading like the dreamy afterimage of a television picture tube switched off in a dark room. His cronies would have been pleased and diverted to know that Gary died with a hard-on.

A day or so later, a new cupola starts to go up on the new wing of the Newall house.

Ω

©'91 Walters

THE CLOTH GODS
OF ZHAMIIR
by Darrell Schweitzer
& Jason van Hollander

Lord Yandi to his Nephew, Prince Lebalan, Greetings.

Zhamiir City, date uncertain, in the Year of the Great Awakening

Beloved Nephew,

What an incredible place! That is the beginning of my explanation, my excuse, if you will — the reason your aged, doddering, and confessedly long-winded Uncle has completed the arduous journey hence, in something resembling secrecy, without even telling you, my confidant Lebalan. Yes, it was urgent. Yes, the greatest secrecy *was* required, for the most astonishing of reasons.

I ramble, I fear.

Zhamiir! The amazing city.

When we entered Zhamiir, we were promptly festooned with reeking-sweet garlands. A thought came to me: *the perfumed corpses of the newly dead, beginning to "go."* It was not quite a pleasant smell. Nothing in Zhamiir is quite pleasant.

Former priests welcomed us at the city gate, professional greeters now. Vendors (former acolytes, says Hesh) swarmed, hawking trinkets, fruits, baubles, chipped and tarnished icons — these latter mere curiosities, no longer holy. Sullen old women (ex-priestesses?) strutted before us in diaphanous costume so we might inspect their dreary wares. And I realized that an entire class has been displaced in Zhamiir. Gone are the priests, gone the temple bell-ringers, the divine seeresses, the ineffably sacrosanct harlots. Gone, all of them, with the introduction of the god-auctions.

"Make way!" the caravan master shouted again and again. He had to raise his stick until a path was cleared. Dizzied by the garlands, we staggered through the granite gate which is the preferred entrance to the famous city of Zhamiir — "where the gods have been subdued," as the new expression goes.

Still the former priests swarmed about us, and my thin-lipped and disapproving Hesh protected his Lord and Master from this beggarly rabble by shooing them away with a big fronded whisk. (Doubtless he was expecting a pipe or two of *hanquil* for his efforts.) I have to laugh, even now, recalling the scene. Hesh is such a droopy, sad clown, as grave as the once-priests themselves.

Throughout our three-week journey he made the most astonishing observations:

"The desert dung-beetles," said he, "have less shame than the slave-deities of Zhamiir. They, at least, roll in shit of their own choosing."

And also: "The sand of the Iracassi, each speck, mocks the vanquished gods."

At a fountain within the city, I ladled sparkling water over my brow, recalling these matchless philosophies. And through this flowing mask, I smiled at the absurdity of all around me. Gods for sale! No more do worshipers make expensive sacrifices in the temples. No more collection baskets. Now gold flows *from* religious observance, not into it. A topsy-turvy world! The thought of it so amazed and pleased me I wanted to dance. The water ran over my ears like a whispery song and I looked around for Hesh, unmerry Hesh.

Soon government clerks surrounded us, thick as flies. Will the Zhamiirites sell off their rulers next? Kings, lords, bureaucrats, the lot? One can only hope.

Many documents were initialed and stamped. Money changed hands. The caravan broke up, the tongueless bearers and their overseer paid off, the camels led away. When it was done Hesh and I sported bronze medallions around our necks, designating us short-term visitors to Zhamiir, *tourists*.

Otherwise we were free. "What's to stop us from going to the auctions this very night?" I asked.

Hesh returned me a troubled gaze, as always when I suggest anything. What a long face he pulled this time! "Bad luck . . . to purchase a god . . . so soon into the city."

"Better check their teeth first, eh?"

"Master, this is a serious occasion."

"I am merely optimistic, my dear Hesh. Merely that. It makes me cheerful. Eager."

We proceeded. In spite of his best efforts, Hesh, poor man, could not prevent two guides from attaching themselves to us. Dwarfs, they were, from somewhere in the bazaar, darting out of the tangles of booths and penned animals and barrels and huge jars and jostling crowds. One moment I had merely Hesh, the next, these two with piping voices and rapid little legs. I couldn't refrain from giggling.

"Master!" my servant hissed. "Your dignity!"

Still I laughed, at Hesh's futile cluckings, at myself (I was fairly drunk with fatigue, and with anticipation), as well as the vagaries of nature which fashion such tiny grotesques.

"*Hanquil* dens, down this alley," the big-browed one announced. "Love may be purchased very reasonably here," intoned the other, making obscene gestures with his stumpy fingers.

"Alas," I sighed. "I am too weary."

"Of course," said the bushy one. "You are well into your years."

"I am a vigorous man!" — I thumped my chest — "Not nearly so old in my appetites as some of the younger men."

"My brother meant no insult," said the smaller dwarf. "You have come to our city for the auctions, I take it."

"Perhaps."

"Ah, a wealthy man," crooned the other, his huge forehead and the hedgerows above his eyes making him seem all the more ridiculous.

"A collector," chirped the smaller, "a connoisseur, come all the way across the Iracassi Desert to purchase one of our poor gods."

The dwarfs looked at me eagerly, awaiting my response, but it was Hesh who spoke, slowly and deliberately, as if addressing a multitude.

"My master has come to Zhamiir to witness the end of the Age of Miracles. Perhaps he will acquire a souvenir, if it pleases him. A token of the Great Awakening . . . the time when men are made free from the gods."

"Takes a lot of money to buy a god, even a little one," the big-browed dwarf observed, bowing, before he produced a feather brush and started dusting my feet.

Thanking them, I threw some newly minted coins (one of which the small dwarf promptly bit), then Hesh and I managed to escape.

I paused, further along, taking deep breaths, that I might sample the exhalations of this fabled city.

The streets, Nephew, the streets! What a riot of color before our eyes, what noises, what spicy stinks! Murmurous crowds, low-hanging banners drooping above us, shops, glass-blowers, soul-merchants, stunning women for the harem, the beautiful, honey-colored children of Zhamiir, all swarming before us like figures on a glorious tapestry. For a time I forgot my exhaustion. Merely being in Zhamiir filled me with frenzied energy. After three weeks in the Iracassi, I can tell you, I was grateful for such a glorious vision.

It was twilight. Shadows filled the rabbit-warren streets, softening contrasts. Sounds grew muted. Intricate lanterns swayed on posts as they were lit, one by one, by a spry old man who sang with the purity of an angel.

Here! Here mankind had triumphed over the gods!

The beauty of it moved me deeply, and I felt that mystical-mercantile stirring which is my gift: I felt the Tears of Imminent Fortune rolling out of my eyes.

"Can't we just peek into one of the auctions?" I pleaded with Hesh, dabbing my eyes with my sash.

He took me by the hand and led me. "Bad luck so soon. Consider all things first, Lord, then act deliberately. Your *enthusiasms* are like summer storms, swift and thunderous and soon gone."

I obeyed him and followed. Sometimes even I forget who is the master and who the servant.

Sleep, dear Nephew, eluded me that first night. At the place where we stayed, a kind of palace for the wealthy traveler, there was much to keep me awake: sighing breezes, occasional shouts or blaring horns from the distant street, Hesh snoring in the adjoining room, flickers from torchlight dancing under the door — and voluptuous grunts that rampaged up the marble halls. This last disturbed me. Almost delirious with fatigue, I flung open the slatted door and beheld the gleaming marble corridor.

In the middle of this hallway I stood, a man of sixty years, half undressed. Then a faint shuffling advanced. A servant appeared, a boy of perhaps ten, thin and terribly frail, with hair as white as the moon.

"Who indulges in love at this hour?" I demanded, nodding in the direction of the sounds.

The boy shrugged at my question. I gazed into his face, into his almost colorless eyes. Something about him fascinated me immensely: his body was all bones and angles and blue veins. He wore only a ragged robe of the same diaphanous stuff the women had worn at the city gate. In the half light, with torches flickering behind him, he seemed somehow less than entirely real, not a solid child of flesh, but an apparition.

I wanted him very much. No, no Nephew, you mustn't think that your old uncle has acquired a new vice. The familiar lusts are enough for me. This was merely the desire to *acquire*. The boy was a treasure. He was beautiful in his strange way, his eyes too wide, his head too large for his shrunken body, his skin like white marble, perfectly smooth, delicately shaped.

He seemed a symbol to me, the final hieroglyph in the mystery of existence. He couldn't be merely a malnourished child. No, that was impossible.

He held a tray, on which were two red, dripping roots. At first I thought they were vegetables, at least. Then it occurred to me that they were bloody claws, torn, not severed, from a bird, probably a peacock.

He placed the tray on a stand beside me. I stared down at it for a moment. When I looked up, the boy was gone. His bare feet had been utterly soundless on the smooth, cold marble.

Revulsed, I emptied the tray into a chamber pot, then stood again alone in the empty corridor. I no longer heard the sounds of passion. There was only silence now. It affected me strangely, this silence. There is a quality, Nephew, about walking in places where men dream. As if in compensation for our dream-loss, we are granted a strange serenity.

Soothed by this very quality, I drifted down a flight of stairs and into a courtyard. There, limned by moonlight, the boy-servant was kneeling, burying something. Ah, but I hadn't meant to spy on him.

"Are you real?" the child asked me all at once.

I wasn't entirely sure. I pinched my wrist and it hurt enough for me to reply, "Yes, real enough." I stifled a yawn. "What a question. Why shouldn't I be real?"

The boy rose to his feet, carefully brushing dirt off his hands and knees, as if to remove anything which might mar his unearthly appearance. "You could be a ghost," he said.

"If the gods are sold in Zhamiir," I teased, "then surely ghosts are given away for free and are found everywhere. You should be used to ghosts by now, and able to recognize one without any hesitation."

He stared at me, utterly unaware of my attempted humor, his eyes wide, bewitching.

"Have you ever seen a ghost?"

"Alas, I have not. In my own country they are reserved for the privileged few. Have you ever seen one?"

"Not of the dead," he said softly, and if embarrassed by the admission, "but of the living."

I asked him to explain what ghosts were.

"Souls without bodies."

"And what are the gods?" *This* question, Nephew, I asked in deepest earnest. My instinct was alive again. Somehow this boy knew. He was an ambassador who moved freely between life and death, my fancy told me, perhaps a native not of this world of living men, but of the other.

"The gods . . ." he began, shifting nervously. He didn't seem to know. Were he merely a child, I would have concluded that he was simply too young, or too frightened of this strange old man who accosted him in the middle of the night, interrupting some secret doing.

To put him at ease I smiled and touched him gently on the shoulder — his flesh was cold — *cold!* — and quoted one of the old poems of Zhamiir, now forbidden: *"The gods are portions of Eternity, ensouled."*

He stood still, gazing up at me inscrutably.

"Do you like poetry, boy?"

"I don't know, Lord."

Cautiously, I toed the burial mound. "What have you buried here?"

"A peacock, sir. What's left of it."

"Eh?"

"Promise you won't tell?"

"I promise."

"I was hungry, Sir. They mistreat me here."

"It was merely that, hunger? Not some secret divination?"

©'91 Walters

For the first time, he seemed afraid of me.

"No, Sir!"

"And the claws? What were you doing with them, in the hall outside my room?"

"I had to get rid of them separately."

"Why, of course," I said calmly, pretending to understand. In truth I hadn't the slightest idea what he was talking about. Another mystery. "What is your name, young man?"

"I am called Nimbulec."

I was beginning to feel the weight of my body and my years. I eased myself onto a marble bench and bade the boy sit beside me. Above us in a tree, some night bird chirped softly. The boy sat, shivering.

"Tell me, Nimbulec. What are the god-auctions like?"

"I only know what I hear, Sir. I'm not allowed out."

"And what do you hear?"

"That the auctions take place in a bazaar that used to be a big temple. The gods are rolled up in carpets and the ends are tied so they can't get out."

The child alluded, of course, in his imperfect and beguiling way, to the ensorcelled carpets of Zhamiir, rugs which thump and crawl, gods trapped inside, but not merely bound inside the carpet, but *woven* there. That is the great secret of Zhamiir, Nephew, the means by which humanity has been liberated. The weavers of the city grew so skilled, so cunning with their threads and their dyes and their patterns, that they could create the very, the true likenesses of the gods in cloth. Thus they bound them, snatching each god out of the air when the image was made in a carpet, binding each god when the last knot was tied. There were, there still are, many, many weavers in Zhamiir. With the help of the people, with the backing of rich patrons, they wove many, many carpets, far more than there were gods. They got them all.

I had heard as much during our trek across the Iracassi. The men of Zhamiir had long been tyrannized by the gods and by their wicked priests. They rose up, a revolution led by weavers and rug-merchants.

I sat still beside the boy, thinking, for once unsure of what I was doing in this place. I had been so firm of purpose when I arrived. Now I was getting muddled.

"I should like to purchase a god, Nimbulec," I said. "If I have enough money left over, I should like to purchase you, too, from your master. Do you have any idea what he paid for you?"

"I was a foundling," the boy said solemnly. "A gift of fortune."

"This is a gift," I told Hesh later, offering him a vial of *hanquil* and a glistening glass pipe, newly purchased. "Take it," I commanded. "You've earned it ten times over. But, I beg you, please don't puff anything until we return from the auction. I need your mind at its sharpest."

Hesh, feigning surprise, lowered his gaze and held open his wide, dusky palm. "Thank you," he intoned, but joylessly, or else he would not have been Hesh.

We were just finishing our dinner. Servants of the house scurried in and out, deferring to Hesh and myself equally, as if we were not master and man, but two guests of similar rank. I looked around for the boy Nimbulec, but did not see him.

The day had been without purpose and without profit. I'd gone into the bazaar, but found little worth haggling over, only trifles, like the pipe and the *hanquil*. So I had returned to the baths, allowing myself to be cleansed and purged. My beard had been curled too, so perfumed with a volatile pomade that I swore I'd burst into flame if I stepped out into the sunlight.

Dear Nephew, that's how wasted the

day was. I was reduced to caring about such matters.

Night would be everything, though, the purpose of our wait, of our wasted day, of the long trek to Zhamiir. With the lowering of the sun, the stone horns of Zhamiir would cry out the triumph of the city, and of man, signaling mockery of the defeated gods. Then the auctions would begin. I waited patiently. My purse was very fat indeed.

Twilight — that superbly evocative hour — had deepened the ruddy sky. It was like blood infused with Divine light, spilled across the face of the cosmos. Thus it affected my mood as Hesh and I trotted toward the auctions.

Even my inscrutable servant's face was given a new hue. He glowed like a man lit from within, a man afire with the stolen emanations of the gods. "The cloth gods of Zhamiir," he muttered as he pushed and shoved our way through the noisy, gaudily-dressed crowd, into the courtyard of a half-destroyed temple, "an entire toppled pantheon, for sale."

A trick of the light confused me: his eyes were dark-orbited pits, pinpointed each with a single, fiery speck.

I paused, a little afraid. For a moment he was not my familiar Hesh at all, but some other kind of being, gazing out through the fleshly form of my servant as one might through a gauze or veil.

Then I shrugged, dismissing the impression as one more strangeness of Zhamiir.

"The gods. I curse the gods," he kept muttering. I could not get him to explain. I think he sensed something too, that the gods were all around us, not bound in cloth at all, but in the air, in the very dust of Zhamiir.

"I curse the gods," he said.

"Weren't you a temple foundling?" I asked, as we made our way under a frowning, bloodlighted arch. "Didn't the gods protect you? Didn't they protect you?"

"My mother abandoned me to the gods, and the gods abandoned me to the riddle-priests with their detestable chants and their insatiable hunger for money. Not as honest as regular merchants either. They gave no good value for their coin."

"Whereas, if one goes to a rug-merchant to buy, one comes away with, at the very least, a serviceable rug."

Oblivious to my delicious irony, he clutched my sleeve as we halted in front of the desecrated fane. "Don't be put off by the auctioneers," he suddenly warned me. "They are priests, god-smitten men, even now. And they wear masks. While you were gone today, I asked many things of the household servants. They told me that the priests wear masks."

"Masks?"

"Their faces have been burned off. The skin of their hands is peeled off as well. Masks of paraffin and gloves of human skin — their own — to spare the sensibilities of the bidders."

I shuddered. I glanced around at the crowd. The people of Zhamiir seemed tense, filled with emotion waiting to burst forth. They were raucous, but this was not a happy crowd. This was no holiday, but, I felt, a ritual of unending vengeance, against the gods, against the priests, against everything vast and magical and beyond the grasp of the individual Zhamiirite.

"But why these particular mutilations?"

"These were the high priests, the true visionaries, not the petty money-grubbers you saw at the city gate yesterday. These men beheld the gods regularly — not merely the stone idols, but the true, spiritual forms — and they spoke with them. They dreamed mighty dreams and spoke prophecies. They made the people of Zhamiir afraid. Therefore the authorities decreed that they should suffer the most, disfigured, being forced to sell their own gods on the auction block. It is thought just."

The crowd heaved forward. Hesh clung to my sleeve as we passed beneath a cracked frieze. A tiny tile fell onto my head, a perfectly blue square of porcelain the size of my fingernail. I turned it over in my hand as if it were a coin, then slipped it in my pocket.

"What did you find, Master?"

"An omen, probably. Are signs and omens also sold in Zhamiir, along with the gods?"

"No, Master. Without the gods to direct them, the omens occur at random. They are worthless."

"Ah."

The courtyard opened into an inner yard, once the sanctuary of the temple and forbidden to all except the priests. Here, many things drew my attention and wonder. Headless statues turned slowly on circular bases, driven by some unseen mechanism, their stone hands waving slowly in the air, beckoning us onward. Numbered plaques dangled from posts. A huge proscenium held the bundled 'wares,' the very gods themselves, while god-beaters stood guard over them with their flails of gold, whose knouts were barbed with the fingerbones of the faithful.

Even here, hucksters were everywhere. Bags of coins on every counter. A Tabernacle of Commerce.

The crowd jeered. They shouted and clapped hands. They blew on obscenely-shaped wooden horns. And many of them put on masks, the visages of hyenas and rats and serpents. Nearby was one with the face of a drooling idiot, but with a third eye in the middle of his forehead. He was triply cross-eyed.

I asked and Hesh explained:

"Thus they mock the priests, whose scabby faces were burnt off."

The noise rose to a crescendo, then dropped to near silence, as some of the actual priests were herded out onto the stage. I could tell they were the disfigured ones immediately. Their masks were not clownish, but somber, almost expressionless, molded of pale white wax.

The silence did not hold, but gave way to rude shouts from the gallery behind us. Ah, the merriment and torment of this place! Black pigs, let loose from somewhere at the back of the stage, ran squealing between the priests' legs. An elderly priest tripped and fell. His mask shattered, and he sat up. Screams from the stage and from the audience. I glimpsed a raw red oval. Then he was led away, a bag over his head. The pigs tumbled down into the crowd. Small boys chased after them, shoving past the adults.

Lamps swung wildly on poles, agitated by the crowd. Underwear and pornographic tapestries flapped from pillars like flags. Someone threw a clown mask toward the stage, sending it whirling over the heads of the priests. Another mask followed, and another.

Then a priest raised his hands and there was *silence*. His mask was not like the others. The mouth of it was huge, grotesquely distorted, like that of a painted clown under torture. As if by magic, at a mere gesture from this one, the *tambangs* and *zootibars* were stilled, these musical instruments placed on laps as, meekly, the crowd settled to the mucid, once-glossy marble floor. You could hear the birds of evening chirruping in the trees once more.

"The foremost of all the high priests," whispered Hesh, "once lord of this city."

"A salute to Abannah," the priest began, his voice very soft, but perfectly audible, like the wind. Behind the translucence of his mask, charred lips writhed like worms. He made references I did not understand, to "souls sold in Tamarack," to "the black ship of Ong-Zwarba," and to "Mung and the sign of Mung," and to "Bel-Hemad, on whose shoulders the birds of the air find rest."

Many of his other words were strange too. He spoke the priest-talk, the religious dialect of the city, now preserved only in ribald jokes, and at these auctions. Hesh translated: ". . . the tutelary deities of the city . . . being soft gods, gods that loved their people, gods who did not allow themselves to be feared, even when they were stern and just."

The silence of the crowd turned to anger. I sensed that these arrogant Zhamiirites were still a little abashed at what they had done, that they did not wish to be reminded of how things had been before the Great Toppling of the city's pantheon.

Rotten vegetables flew at the doddering once-priest. His mask was broken by the impact of one of these missiles, and he staggered back, his ruined forehead bare. He crashed into the wooden racks and a single, gorgeously embroidered carpet tumbled into the stage with a thud, then wriggled slightly.

A god-beater stepped forward, his flail upraised, but the priest fell to his knees, trembling, and kissed the rolled cloth with his waxen lips. As he knelt, an assistant gingerly tied a yellow sash around the old man's head, binding his broken mask in place, concealing his seared flesh once more.

"Start the bidding!" the crowd shouted, again and again, making it a chant. "Start! Start! Start!"

"Look," I whispered to Hesh. "The old priest weeps. This is a cruel thing, no matter how wicked he once was."

"He cannot weep, Master. His tearducts were burned away."

A wind arose from nowhere, whirled about the former holy of holies, choking us with dust. I felt, for an instant, a presence, as if a thousand ghosts were rushing by, turning, rushing again. I shivered.

"Lord?" a voice from my left side called. I turned, surprised. Hesh sat on my right. For just an instant, the boy Nimbulec was there. I touched him. *Cold.*

"What are you doing here?"

"I?" said Hesh. "I accompany you. To witness this spectacle, and perhaps to acquire a cast-off divinity."

I whirled. "Not you. Him." I turned back to where the boy had been. He was gone. The people nearby gazed intently at the stage, unperturbed.

"What is it?" said Hesh.

"Didn't you see him?"

It was clear he had not.

The auction proceeded. First the carpet which had fallen was auctioned off. I went to raise my hand, to bid, but Hesh tugged on my sleeve.

"It is never wise to bid on the first," he said, but others did, and the carpet went to a huge black man clad in gold. His fair-skinned servants bore the thing away. I thought I heard the captive god whimper.

Soon I perceived that the pantheon of Zhamiir was a vast and unequal one, and that the hierarchic standing of each god is displayed by the weave and design, as well as sheer yardage. Gods with some significance are sold in bolts of brilliantly-patterned twill, the ends tied with special silver or golden cord. Lesser deities are rolled in cylinders of garish fabric, fantastically patterned. Godlets, demi-gods, demiurges, and the like are wrapped in mats, curtains, or even scarves.

But the prices brought by each divinity were not necessarily relative to the size of the carpets, or the finery. There was a pattern here, which I could not divine. Yes, a loaded word that.

For once I broke away from Hesh, and placed a bid on a carpet rolled long and thin like a snake, and pale green, without any exterior design. That one, perhaps —

But I was defeated.

"No, Master. It was not the correct one for you," said Hesh.

I bid again and lost.

"Nor that. Please wait. Do not throw your money away."

"How does anyone *know?*"

"Perhaps by chance. Much is left to chance in a city not ruled by gods. Perhaps the gods themselves call out to their new masters. Perhaps they manifest themselves, like foundlings on a temple doorstep."

Hesh, strangely, was weeping.

Around us the crowd hooted and jeered as each new carpet was brought out, stood on end, and its provenance described.

"A god of hearths and fires," said the priest. "Good for the wife and children. Good for keeping your feet warm in the winter." (Oh! How he visibly winced to make these witticisms! Surely a torturer had written the speech for him.)

Still more gods came onto the block, many crawling across the stage, hunching like huge worms while the beaters whacked them. Strange, glittering dust rose.

"The god-dust," Hesh told me. "The last remnant of the power of the fallen ones. See how it rises like smoke."

Moans emanated from the carpets, like nothing else heard on the Earth, aetheric squeals, the last babblings of the helpless, senile gods of Zhamiir.

Still bids were called out. Plaques on pillars were flipped over to the next number, and the auction continued.

"When?" I whispered.

"I know not. Perhaps not this time. Perhaps never."

For once my precious Hesh was wrong, truly wrong. The time came. I knew it. I had gazed down at my purse, then opened it, peering in at the golden royals within. Then I looked up, and to my astonishment beheld the gaunt, pale boy Nimbulec on the stage beside the priest. He had his hand on the current offering — a plain brown carpet with no markings, bound in ordinary rope — steadying it, as if he were the priest's assistant. No one else seemed to have noticed him. He smiled directly at me.

I leapt to my feet.

"That one!" I cried. "I'll take it!" I offered all that I had, so vehemently that no one opposed me. The priest, startled, acquiesced quickly.

The boy Nimbulec had vanished somewhere.

Still the crowd hooted and gibbered. Still the priest made his painful speeches. But I paid no more attention to the events of the evening. I sat down, contented.

"Have you done right, Master?" Hesh asked. He seemed afraid. He genuinely didn't know.

"Patterns," Hesh mused as we carried the thumping, wriggling carpet through the near empty streets. "Unceasing repetitions call forth the gods. Chanting will do it."

"Unceasing repetition will also bind them," I said, "as it has in our prize."

"The subtle designs in a carpet, any carpet, even a seemingly plain one, the mirrored strands, the sidereal weft, and" — he paused for a deep breath and continued, most solemnly — "the looms, the worm-driven looms that spin for centuries in incantatory rhythms. All these things the gods confuse for devotion."

"The prayers of the priests," I said, "echoing down the great roadway of time, repeating, repeating —"

"— a thrumming which the gods sense, which draws them, which nourishes them —"

The center of our carpet sagged. We nearly lost our grip on it. Hesh struck it underhanded with a golden flail which had come with our purchase — "an added benefit," the priest had said, "for one so generous" — and it straightened itself and even seemed to grow lighter.

"Ah, time," I said. "Vibrations which *accumulate through time* and bring the gods to us, the sigils which draw them down."

So we walked through the dark streets, our speech distracted and strange. I hardly knew what we were saying or what was meant. It was as if some others spoke through the two of us, babbling in their own secret code. But it all fit, like the revealed wisdom that comes to the drunkard or the *hanquil*-addict in his delirium, only to evaporate like a misty dream in the bright morning.

It was only as we reached our rooms that my mind cleared. I began to worry about finances. Had I overspent impulsively? Would we even have enough to pay for our rent and our passage back home? I worried about thieves too, about the long journey itself, about accidentally tearing our own aged guts from the weight of our treasure.

Exhausted, we dumped the carpet unceremoniously on the floor. Hesh fetched cool wine from the kitchen. I sat still, regarding the still form before me. Once it had been placed on the floor, the carpet did not whimper or move. It seemed merely a roll of cloth.

But I knew better. I cannot truly express, dear Nephew, how I felt just then, exhausted but trembling in my final expectation.

I have not made it clear precisely *why* I had come to Zhamiir, why I had done this thing.

I can only try to express it in words. The mere strokes of the pen are not enough. The utterances of the voice are like grains of sand flung into the air by a child trying to cover up the sky that way. Verily.

I think some folk purchase gods in Zhamiir out of sheer self-exaltation. They do it to show that they are greater than gods. How better to show one's own grandiosity than to have a former divinity of field or forest nailed to one's wall or floor? Surely a general would be pleased to furnish his tent with a god of war.

That is one reason. Another is superstitious. People think these fallen gods will bring them good fortune. But this is illogical, even as it is illogical for our own countrymen to believe, as so many do, that the tail of the *hata*-lizard is lucky — for all the good luck that particular lizard enjoyed! Similarly, if the gods had any luck to spare, they would not be in such a ridiculous state.

The third reason is more intimate, more personal, more vague. It is as much a mystery as anything celebrated in the darkened temples of old. There are those who, for all they do not respect the gods, seek the divine, for themselves. What fascination, what uniquely personal glory, to hold in one's hand that which is, or was formerly, divine.

Such persons wish to draw the essence of the gods into their own souls, to gain wisdom, or power, or whatever it is the gods have to offer, to become, in a sense, gods themselves. This is done at a great price, surely, so those who purchase a god of Zhamiir with such a goal in mind take on a greater burden than any weight of cloth. They may despise the priests, the temples, the money-grubbing of organized religion, but they are secretly as god-mad as any whose face was flayed away.

In that way I too am mad, Nephew. Because I am old, because I am near to death, I seek news from that far country into which I will soon journey. Because the gods are immortal, even the gods of Zhamiir, I hoped they could provide me with some glimpse. At the least, they could grant me something akin to wisdom, so that my life might have its proper culmination, like a deal rightly concluded, like the particularly deft final line of a poem. I did not seek immortality for myself, but merely assurance.

I do not think the people of Zhamiir can understand that, nor can Hesh, nor can even you, my dear Nephew. But ponder it. It is my reason.

Therefore I bought the carpet that I might lie on it, and sleep, and dream, and in my dreams the god within the weave might make himself known to me.

Therefore I waited, breathing hard. Hesh returned with the wine, and I drank. It soothed me.

"Slowly, Master. Slowly."

I swallowed.

"Have we any money left?"

"A little, Master."

"Good. Then I want you to make a second purchase. Now."

"*Now?* What can be so important that you must have it now, at this hour of the night."

"Trust me, good Hesh. I know. Go rouse the master of the house. Then purchase the boy Nimbulec and bring him to me."

It was my intention that Nimbulec should lie beside me on the carpet as I slept, so that whatever wisdom I might gain from the god would be passed on to him, and my explorations of the Beyond would not perish with me. I wanted to make the boy my apprentice in the understanding of Death. I felt certain that he would be naturally talented in this endeavor.

Hesh paused, as if embarrassed to speak.

"What is it?" I said.

"Master, as it happens, when I went for the wine the steward of the kitchens asked me if I had seen that very Nimbulec. It seems the child has run off."

"Then we shall proceed without him," I said, hiding my disappointment.

So Hesh and I cut the ropes which bound the carpet and unrolled it, slowly revealing an extremely intricate, albeit badly faded pattern in the cloth.

And something else.

Hesh was the first to cry out.

Then I, too, screamed and fell to my knees, hiding my face with my hands like a priest who had lost his mask. But I looked through my fingers and saw what was there: it was Nimbulec, horribly beaten, his gauzy robe melted into his blood and torn flesh like a huge scab. For an instant yet he was still alive. He turned toward me. Our eyes met, his glassy with pain. Then his flesh fell away even as I watched, crumbling like grains trickling from an hourglass. His skeleton was fantastically delicate, like a tracery of spun glass, like a spider's web. When it was gone too, all that remained was some dust, and the old, shrivelled claws of a bird.

Numbly, Hesh and I unrolled the carpet the rest of the way. In the dim light we could barely make out the overall pattern of the weave. The threads were brown and black, the lighter against the darker revealing the image of a god, who was like a bird with the face of a solemn, gaunt child who stared at us with wide, pain-filled eyes.

I understood nothing then, nothing at all, but I knew what I had to do. I dismissed Hesh for the night. He was reluctant to leave, but I bade him sleep outside my door.

Then I lay down on the dusty carpet and tried to sleep, to call the dreams of the god into my own mind. As I lay there, my fingers played idly with the shrunken bird-feet until the feet broke like old twigs.

What followed was not a dream. I am sure of it. It was a true thing, which really happened.

The child Nimbulec sat beside me where I lay. He was naked now. He sat up, out of his ruined gown, passing through it like smoke. I touched him on the knee. Still his flesh was as cold and hard as marble.

I babbled. "My boy, how would you like to come and work for me? My nephew is a rich merchant-prince. We live together in a great house, where there are many servants like yourself, a whole community of them, with children your own age. We work our servants hard, but we

feed them well, and there are no beatings."

"And if they are false to you, Master?" said he.

"Then, most reluctantly, we sell them."

"As all things are sold, Master."

"Yes, as all things are sold."

Without another word, he rose and left the room. I sat up, startled, the hurried after him.

Somehow I knew it would be useless to call for Hesh.

I ran. Once I caught a glimpse the boy — a flash of white in the moonlight — as he vanished among pillars. Again, as he turned a corner. Again as he flickered through a doorway, into the courtyard where he had buried the peacock.

Onward, into the city. A waxenmasked priest passed us in the street, singing a dirge, ringing a little bell. I ran, gasping in the suddenly chill night air, reminded of my own mortality. What if my very heart burst? There are physi-

cians in Zhamiir, yes, but I had little money with which to pay them, and there is no charity in a city were the gods are auctioned off. Into the desert. The sands of the Iracassi swirled around us in a sudden storm. I lost sight of the boy. Then the storm passed. The air was clear once more. Now the silence was absolute, even the sand asleep and dreaming.

It seemed that I ran across an ocean of night, a sea of sand, as phantasmical tides surged around me, as dusty surf boiled around my ankles, withdrawing as waves were spent, drawing me onward, downward, out of the world of living men.

It seemed that glowing skeletons of men and beasts rose and fell slowly in the sand, swimming like fish.

Then I heard Nimbulec, far ahead, singing the priest's dirge.

I came to the top of a dune. Thousands of brilliantly colored birds rose up in my face, peacocks, pheasants, hawks, their wings thundering, like an incredible tidal wave of wildly undulating flowers, flame-colored, paradise-tinted.

Then they were gone, and Nimbulec stood before me, his hands apart, as if he had just released all those birds. I knew that he had.

I heard a voice speaking from the sky. It sounded like Hesh. *Will we ever recover the gods, recover them truly, and bring them into the world once again?*

Now shapes like crabs rose out of the sand, but their faces were those of men, and more than men, ancient, inscrutable, implacable.

"Nimbulec!" I shouted.

He smiled when he saw me. He looked up, at star-silvered gulfs. The sky surged like another, incomprehensible sea.

"You will not recover the gods," he said, his voice impossibly loud, inside my mind, "because you have never truly lost them. You reasoned correctly, old man of a foreign country, when you concluded that the dust rising from the carpet was the power of the god bound therein. The gods have never departed from Zhamiir. They are in the very air, in the very dust. The people breathe them with every breath, filling their lungs with miracles."

He walked toward me. Once more I saw that his body was fantastically delicate, his skin a pale tracery of blue veins. The light of the newly-risen, waning moon shone through him clearly, and he cast no shadow.

He took me by the hand, and, yes, his touch was very cold, of the grave.

"Come with me now, and journey into the dark land," he said. "This is the meaning of your coming to the city. Your every act was an omen. Everything manipulated you to this end."

"Master," I said, very deliberately calling him that, this child whom I had once wanted half as a servant, half as a curiosity the way one might collect strangely-shaped shells. "Master, at the end, at the very end, I find that I am afraid."

"Come," he said. "Leave your fear behind like an old cloak."

Naked, I ran beside him, my body young and vigorous as it has not been in thirty years. I ran, down a gray slope of ash, down, out of the world, through those gates through which the dead souls pass, down into the other land, where the souls of my ancestors rose up out of a marsh to greet me, where a black castle filled the sky and the few, strange stars were the torches flickering in its windows; down, past the great dragon that waits, down into the swirling chaos, into nothingness, which is neither darkness nor light, neither thunder nor silence.

And all the wisdom I ever sought and feared came to me, and all the glory. I had reached the end of my curiosity, of my fascination.

But here is the most exquisite irony of all, dearest Nephew. I had never died. Not quite, not yet.

Shortly before dawn Hesh disobeyed my order and came into the room. I don't know what he saw exactly, but in sudden alarm he dragged me off the carpet.

I awoke later in the sickbed where I now lie. I am filled with pain. My mind is dimmed, like a lamp guttering out. In my lucid intervals, between pain and delirium, I am able to write.

I cannot describe what I saw. Not truly. All I can say is that, indeed, the gods of Zhamiir are everywhere, in the air I breathe. I exhale miracles and revelations. The vulgarity of the people here, the lewdness, the anger, the mockery — all these things are masks, like the waxen masks of the priests. Beneath them are the mutilated, god-burned, god-crazed folk of the city, who have magnificently, foolishly, incredibly torn down the hierarchy of the gods, spilling the divine power out of the temples where, in other lands, it is safely contained like boiling pitch in a pot. In

Zhamiir men have been scalded by it, every last one of them.

Hesh enters with fresh pens and parchment.

"Write if it comforts you, Master," he says. "I fear you may not last long. The strain of the running was too much for you."

"The running? How do you know about that?"

"I had a dream, Master. I saw you go."

"A dream sent by a god, a revelation?"

He will not answer that. I cannot ask him about gods and men, about the land beyond life, about the strange ocean in the desert.

I ask what has become of Nimbulec.

"That is very strange, Master. The innkeeper says that they did have a servant boy, who killed a peacock, was beaten for it, and ran away. But he was not like you described. No one has seen a child like that."

"What happens now, Hesh?"

At the end he is like a parent to me. I seek comfort from him. I long for his firm strength.

He is deeply moved, for a long time, unable to speak.

"Master, when I found you, I listened to your heartbeat. It is weak and irregular."

"And the gods are only drawn by a steady beat which never varies. Is that it?"

"I think so, My Lord Yandi."

Ah, Nephew, my heart burns like a torch in my chest —

Ω

A STREET WAS CHOSEN

by Ramsey Campbell

A street was chosen. Within its parameters, homes were randomly selected. Preliminary research yielded details of the occupants as follows:

A (husband, insurance salesman, 30; wife, 28; infant daughter, 18 months)

B (widow, 67)

C (husband, 73; wife, 75; son, library assistant, 38)

D (mother, bank clerk, 32; daughter, 3)

E (husband, social worker, 35; wife, social worker, 34)

F (electrician, male, 51; assistant, male, 25)

G (husband, 42; wife, industrial chemist, 38; son, 4; infant son, 2)

H (mother, 86; son, teacher, 44; son's wife, headmistress, 41; granddaughter, 12; grandson, 11)

I (window-cleaner, male, 53)

J (tax officer, female, 55)

K (milkman, male, 39)

L (waiter, 43)

It was noted that subjects I-L occupied apartments in the same house. Further preliminary observation established that:

(a) subject B wrote letters to newspapers

(b) the children of couples A and G visited each other's homes to play

(c) granddaughter H sat with child D while mother D was elsewhere on an average of 1 evening per week

(d) husband G experienced bouts of temporary impotence lasting between 6 and 8 days

(e) elder F performed sexual acts with his partner in order to maintain the relationship

(f) subject L had recently been released into the community after treatment for schizophrenia

It was decided that stimuli should be applied gradually and with caution. During an initial 8-night period, the following actions were taken:

(1, i) each night a flower was uprooted from the garden of subject B, and all evidence of removal was erased

(1, ii) the lights in house H were caused to switch on at random intervals for periods of up to 5 minutes between the hours of 3 and 6 in the morning

(1, iii) on alternate nights, subject J was wakened shortly after entering deep sleep by telephone calls purporting to advertise life insurance

(1, iv) the tinfoil caps of milk-bottles delivered to subject D were removed after delivery, and feeding nipples substituted

At the end of 8 days, it was noted that subject B was less inclined than previously to engage her neighbours in conversation, and more prone to argue or to take offence. From the 7th day onwards she was seen to spend extended periods at the windows which overlooked her garden.

Subjects F were employed by couple H to trace the source of an apparent electrical malfunction. It was observed that mother H became increasingly hostile to her son's wife both during this process and after electricians F had failed to locate any fault in the wiring. Observations suggested that she blamed either her daughter-in-law or her grandchildren for tampering with the electricity in order to disturb her sleep.

Subject J was observed to approach Subject A in order to obtain names and addresses of insurance companies which advertised by telephone. It was noted that when the list provided by A failed to yield the required explanation, A undertook to make further enquiries on J's behalf.

It was observed that subject D initially responded to the substitution of nipples as if it were a joke. After 2 days, however, she was seen to accuse subject K of the substitution. At the end of the 8-day period she cancelled the delivery and ordered milk from a rival company. It was decided to discontinue the substitution for an indefinite period.

After observations were completed, the following stimuli were applied during a period of 15 days:

(2, i) An anonymous letter based on a computer analysis of B's prose style was published in the free newspaper received by all subjects, objecting to the existence of househusbands and claiming that the writer was aware of two people who committed adultery while their children played together

(2, ii) Every third night as subject L walked home, he was approached by religious pamphleteers whose faces had been altered to resemble the other tenants of his building in the order I, K, J, I, K

(2, iii) The dustbin of subjects F was overturned, and pages from a magazine depicting naked prepubertal boys were scattered around it

(2, iv) The figure of subject I was projected on the bedroom window of subjects E and caused to appear to pass through it while husband E was alone in the room

(2, v) Brochures advertising old folks' homes were sent on alternate days to son C

(2, vi) Telephone calls using a simulation of the voice of subject J were made

between 3 and 5 in the morning on 6 occasions to house A, complaining that J had just received another advertising call

At the end of the second period of stimuli, the following observations were made:

After the appearance of the letter in the newspaper, husband G was observed to suffer a bout of impotence lasting 11 days. It was also noted that subject D attempted to befriend wives A and G, who appeared to be suspicious of her motives. As a result of this encounter, increasing strain was recorded within couples A and G.

Subject L was seen to examine the mail addressed to subjects I, J, and K, and also to attempt to view the apartments of these subjects through the keyholes. Whenever any two of these subjects began a conversation while L was in the building, attempts by L to overhear were observed. Also noted was the growing tendency of L to scrutinise the faces of diners while he waited on them in the restaurant.

After the elder of subjects F discovered the pages which had apparently been hidden in the dustbin, several disagreements of increasing length and violence between subjects F were recorded, both subjects accusing the other of responsibility for the material. At the end of 11 days, the younger of the subjects was seen to take up residence beyond the parameters of the present experiment. It was further observed that mother G required her sons to promise to inform her or their father if they were approached in any way by subjects F.

It was noted that subject E did not mention the apparition of subject I to his wife.

After the first delivery of brochures to their son, parents C were observed to cease speaking to him, despite his denial of responsibility for the receipt of the material. It was noted that parents C opened and destroyed all brochures subsequently delivered. Hot meals prepared for son C were left on the table for him for up to 1 hour before his consumption of them.

Husband A was seen twice to request subject J not to telephone his house after 11 o'clock at night. When the calls continued, wife A was observed to threaten J with legal action, despite J's denial of all knowledge. During this confrontation, subject L was seen to accuse J of attempting to distress both himself and wife A. It was recorded that wife A advised him to take up the matter with the landlord of the apartments.

A decision was reached to increase the level of stimuli. The following actions were taken during a 6-day period:

(3, i) In the absence of subject B, all the furniture in her house was dismantled

(3, ii) Several brochures concerning euthanasia and the right to die were addressed to son C

(3, iii) Whenever husband G succeeded in achieving an erection, the car alarm of subjects A was made to sound

(3, iv) A box of fireworks labelled as a free sample was delivered to children H. Several fireworks were later removed and were exploded inside the house of subject F

(3, v) The face of subject B was made to appear above the beds of children G. When infant G fled, he was caused to fall downstairs. Snapping of the neck was observed to occur

(3, vi) Live insects were introduced into meals which subject L was about to serve to diners

(3, vii) The outer doors of apartments I and K were painted crimson overnight

During and after this period, the following observations were made:

After parents C were seen to examine the brochures addressed to their son, it was noted that they placed his belongings outside the house and employed a neighbour to change the external locks. It was observed that when on his return son C attempted to protest that he owned the house, he was refused any response. Later he was found to be sleeping in a public park. Information was received that when his workmates attempted to counsel him he quit his job. It was observed that although mother C wished to take the son's belongings into the house, father C insisted on their remaining outside.

Grandmother H was seen to attack grandchildren H under the impression that they were responsible for the damage to house F, although the police had accepted evidence that the children could not have been involved. When mother H defended her children from their grandmother, it was noted that she was accused of having succeeded professionally at the expense of her husband. A protracted argument between all five subjects H was observed, after which increases in tension between all subjects were recorded, the greatest increase being between son and wife.

It was observed that when granddaughter H offered to sit with child D, mother D refused to employ her. Mother H was later seen to accuse mother D of attempting to befriend families in the hope of developing a sexual relationship with the father.

Husband G was observed to destroy the headlights of car A with a hammer. The ensuing altercation was seen to be terminated when wife G reported that infant G had been injured on the stairs. It was noted that infant G died en route to the nearest hospital.

It was recorded that subject L was unable to determine whether or not the insects placed in the meals he was about to serve were objectively real. It was noted that this confusion caused L to lose his job. Subsequently L was observed to attempt to persuade several of the other subjects that a pattern was discernible in the various recent events, without success. It was noted that L overheard subjects I and K suggesting that L had repainted their doors.

Surviving child G was seen to inform its parents that subject B had driven infant G out of the children's room. It was observed that when mother G confronted B with this, B accused G of having caused the apparition by experimenting on the children with drugs produced in the laboratory where G worked. It was further noted that subjects E attempted to intervene in the argument but were met with hostility bordering on accusation, both by B and G and by several bystanders. When subject I was attracted by the confrontation, husband E was observed to take refuge in house E.

It was noted that subject L approached his landlord and tried to persuade him that subjects I, J, and K were conspiring against L. It was further observed that when L was given notice to quit the apartment, L set fire to the building in the absence of the other tenants. Temperatures in excess of 450 degrees Celsius were recorded, and it was observed that L was trapped beneath a fallen lintel. Melting of the flesh was seen to precede loss of consciousness, and death was subsequently observed.

Husband E was seen to propose a separation from wife E while refusing to explain his motives. The separation was observed to take place and to become permanent.

Preparations for suicide by subject B were observed. It was noted that the previously dismantled chair used by B for support gave way as the subject was seen to decide against this course of action. Dislocation of the neck by hanging was recorded, and death from strangulation ensued after a period of 53 minutes 27 seconds. It was further observed that after 8 days subject F entered house B and discovered the corpse of subject B.

Because of the risk of discovery, it was decided to discontinue the experiment at this stage. Since the results were judged to be inconclusive, it is proposed that several further experiments on larger groups of subjects should be conducted simultaneously. Communities have been chosen at random, and within them a further random selection of streets has been made.   Ω

THE HOUSE ON THE CLIFF

It crouches there, that house of fears,
    Upon the dark and wooded rise;
    Its gables, gaunt against gray skies,
Jut like a great cat's listening ears.

Upon three sides the woodlands fold
    About its lowering, stone-built walls,
    While on the west a precipice falls
To rushing waters dark and cold.

The country folk who homeward fare
    Shun its environs while the night
    Damps down the sunset's fading light
And owl-calls tremble on the air.

None knows just what those rustics dread —
    There is no vague and vulgar tale
    Of sheeted specters faint and pale,
Of corpses rising from the dead —

Yet some who've braved the late, lone hours
    At certain seasons of the year
    Maintain in trembling tones of fear
That ghost-lights limn those grim, dark towers;

While others, in the autumn time
    When river waters slack their flow,
    Have seen black cave-mouths gape below
And great, webbed footprints in the slime.

Some tell of nights when distant cries
    Reminded them of vanished kin —
    Yet none made bold to go within
Those woods whose branches mask the skies.

O Traveller, seek not to know
    The secrets of that house of gloom
    Whose cat-eared turrets darkly loom
Against the sunset's blood-red glow.

—**Richard L. Tierney**

PATTERNS

by Juleen Brantingham

She never again dreamed of dancing.

There was movement, naturally; patterns formed, broke, reformed in color and light, streaming, whirling, always with grace, but not in the movements of the dance.

Someone who knew little of dancers might have thought it too much to hope to control dreams, but the apparent freedom of the dance is founded in rigid control; the discipline that permits such grace comes first from the mind. She would put it from her, never dream of it again, never ache for what was lost.

But she had lived for this since she was eight years old. Every act, every thought had been somehow related to her training. She had nothing now but pain and emptiness. And Richard. She did not even have herself because if she was no longer a dancer she did not know who she was.

He showed her. There would be something more. They would go away and they would build it together.

It was late July and heat had settled into the valleys like liquid in a cup. All morning she had tried to distract herself, to ignore the heat. Before moving south she had always thought of mountains as cool but this was the humidity of a lowland swamp, the heat of New York at its worst. While Richard was getting ready for work Anya had come out to the shop to throw open the windows, hoping for a breeze. But there was no breeze, no clouds, nothing but the pitiless glare of the sun. When he kissed her goodbye he fingered the damp tendrils at the back of her neck, making her shiver.

She was sitting at her work table when Elizabeth arrived to sweep and dust, to rearrange the quilts on the displays. The girl gossiped about the people of Drover Trail, giving her shy looks. There was a half-finished quilt lying slack on the frame, a Log Cabin pattern in shades of green, but she couldn't bear to work at something so heavy in this weather. She had been cutting pieces for a Double Wedding Ring but she pushed them aside. They were behaving perversely, sticking to each other, depositing a layer of furry lint on her hands.

She remembered the treasure of old silk she'd found in a secondhand shop weeks before. Silk promised coolness and though she knew it was an illusion, she asked Elizabeth to bring her the box from the closet in the house. She started with the shears, cutting away seams and button rows.

"Too hot to be working today. You should be setting in the shade sipping a cold drink." He spoke from the door, surveying the room like a monarch, thumbs tucked into his gun belt.

"So should you. What could be so important that it takes you away from that air-conditioned office?"

Tom Dawson crossed the shop with ponderous dignity, as if claiming it for his own.

"Air-conditioned?" he scoffed. "You talking about the little fan we got and the glass of icewater we set in front of it?" He reached for her hand, then pulled back his own and wiped it on his shirt, which was sweat-stained, spattered, too, with what looked like dried blood.

"What have you been doing?"

"Oh, I been up the hill a ways," he said, sounding disgusted.

The "hill" he referred to was what Anya would have called a mountain. She wondered where Tom came from. Though he softened the endings of his words, his accent wasn't quite the same as Elizabeth's. He'd taken a fatherly interest in Anya and Richard, even telling Richard who to see about the loan they needed to open Anya's shop, but other than his occupation, his life was a mystery.

"Old man had himself a place up there in the woods. One of our local crazies. Guess you could say he got what he deserved."

Anya pressed her lips together and looked at him, laughing silently. He shook his head in rueful agreement, sighed, and started over.

"This old man had buncha dogs. Kept them chained up, starved them, beat them, it looked like, just for the pure joy of having something that couldn't hurt him back. 'Cept one of them did. One of them tore his throat out sometime yesterday, then broke its chain and got away. Neighbor complained about the others howling, was how I found out. Came to warn you to keep your doors shut." Anya started to object but he raised his voice and wouldn't let her get a word in. "Keep 'em shut and keep a watch on your yard. You see a strange dog hanging around, you call me right away."

"It's that dangerous, you think?"

He sighed again. "I don't know, to tell you the truth. Could be so weak it crawled off to die. The others I found, three of them was so bad off I had to put them out of their misery. Even the ones I brought down, don't know what's going to be done with them. A dog that's treated like that, he never gets over it. Turns vicious. When you least expect it he'll jump you and tear your head off." He gave her a one-finger salute and left, closing the door.

Elizabeth was wide-eyed.

"Put up the **Closed** sign and lock the door. Nobody will want to look at quilts in a stuffy shop. We'll go to the house."

"I'll get my things and go on home," the girl said.

"You're not going to walk that road with a dangerous dog on the loose. Richard can take you. Or you can call your father. If you think he can drive this time of day." She hadn't meant to sound critical but everyone knew Elizabeth's father was in a drunken stupor by noon. "You can look at my scrapbook," she added, and was rewarded with a smile. She picked up her canes and began the awkward process of getting to her feet.

No storm came through to cool the air, and sunset brought little relief. Richard suggested dinner out and a movie but even for the promise of air-conditioning it didn't seem worth the trouble. Anya spent the evening going through her pattern books, trying to decide how to use the silk. She kept imagining she heard noises; if it hadn't been so difficult to get up she would have gone to the window a dozen times.

Richard was watching television, the sound turned low. When she noticed he'd fallen asleep, she didn't move to wake him, only smiled, feeling tenderness. He was a quiet man whose manner was sometimes mistaken for a lack of ambition. But he'd had ambitions, once. He gave them up for her, to practice his legal skills here where there was little call for them.

Was that a whisper or a breeze? This time she had to know. Richard woke and came to stand beside her, gazing out at the moonlight. He slipped an arm around her, his cheek brushing her hair.

"Pretty isn't it," he said.

Not even a shadow moved. Why, then, did she have the feeling of being watched? She shivered.

"What's wrong?"

"It's still wild up here, isn't it? Parts of it."

He laughed, tightening his embrace. "Only a city girl could think of this place as wild."

"But there are —" She swallowed. "— bears in the woods?"

"You're afraid of that dog, aren't you?"

"Not afraid exactly." The rest of it came in a rush. "He must be so angry! To be chained up, starved, tormented. To be strong and healthy once and then so helpless." She caught herself then, only then, after revealing too much.

If he understood, he bore it in silence.

She never dreamed of dancing. But there was movement: colors whirled and streamed, patterns formed, broke, re-formed, as in a kaleidoscope: Wheel of Fortune, Country Roads, Castle Walls, Starry Pavement.

She woke with a start. She could still see the shapes, the final pattern: rays and arrows of color as if from a blazing eye, God's Eye. In her dream it had been more than a pattern in patchwork; it had an almost sorcerous power. She slipped from bed, trying not to waken Richard and walked through the house to the shop. She didn't turn on a light but opened the door, allowing moonlight to flood the room. She brought the silk, scissors, and pincushion to the front where the light was bright.

God's Eye was an easy pattern she had made before, but in her dream there had been something odd about the center, a folded look she could not recall clearly. She cut and basted, forgetting time, forgetting the heat. Dissatisfied with the result, she ripped out her stitches and started again. Her mind provided the colors moonlight leached away.

The largest piece of silk was an evening gown — must be, though when she'd pulled it from the rack in the store she thought she'd smelled orange blos-soms, along with decades of mustiness. The hand-stitching, the embroidered bands on sleeves and hem, the hundreds of bugle beads hinted this was no ordinary gown but something crafted with hopes and dreams. But why would someone make a wedding gown of sable-colored silk? Still, as she'd worked with it, she had thought of weddings and of promises made with the knowledge, so its color testified, that even in bright beginnings there is the certainty of sorrow to come.

The other pieces were not unusual, blouses, a skirt, and a scarf, in autumn colors. It would make a striking patch-work.

She knew when she had found the right combination of colors, when she'd found the trick of folding the center. Something clicked. It was the same as in her dream and it had a kind of power. Too excited then to sleep, she had to see how it would look when several blocks were assembled. Hours passed and she didn't notice the sky lighten. She saw nothing but the pattern until she straightened to ease the ache in her back.

She saw the dog.

Her chest was suddenly tight. How long had he been there, leaning against the door? Why hadn't she heard him panting? His tongue was hanging out, dripping drool, and his eyes were glazed with pain. His fur was dark brown but thinned by bad health. She could have counted his ribs but not his wounds, some scabbed, some pus-filled, some raw and bleeding. He was a large dog and even now, starving, must have weighed as much as she did.

The pattern and the colors danced before her eyes. She felt no fear. She should have, she knew, but it simply wasn't there.

She went to him and touched his head, placing her fingers on the only un-wounded part of it, between his ears. She felt a fever's heat. And something more. Something she couldn't name.

Richard stopped, his face frozen in mid-yawn. Beneath the kitchen table the dog lifted his head, his growl a deep rumble. Richard didn't move.

"Stop that," Anya ordered.

The dog dropped his head back to the floor, closed his eyes. Still Richard didn't move.

"What the Hell have you done?" Softly, almost in awe.

"Come and sit down. He's not going to bother you."

He took the cup of coffee she poured but he wouldn't sit and he never took his eyes from the dog.

"Have you called Tom yet?"

"No," she said. "You can if you want. I suppose he should know so people can leave their doors open again. But no one is taking Casey away from me."

He didn't ask about the name and she couldn't have told him. It was his name, that's all.

She wasn't a fighter, never had been. Her battles had always been within herself. Tell her there were rules, she would obey them. Put a block in her path, she would turn back; she wouldn't go around. When the doctors said she would never again walk without pain, she accepted it; she didn't look for miracles.

She fought that day, for Casey's life.

"Anya, get away from him. He killed a man."

Tom stood just inside the front door, his hand inches from his holstered weapon, Richard by his side.

"Self-defense," she said. "You're not taking my dog."

"He's got to be put down. He's dangerous."

"Self-defense," she repeated.

"Anya, we're talking about a dog. I'm sorry as Hell about what that old man did. If I'd known in time I'd a found a way to stop it. But it's done and he killed the man. He's turned vicious. He can't ever be trusted."

"Look at him," she said, turning to look herself. He gazed up at her with adoring eyes, as if she were a candle burning in the darkest night of his life.

"Means nothing," Tom said. "He was hurt and you made him feel better. He's still weak. When he's healthy again, when someone does something that reminds him of how he was hurt before, he's going to defend himself. Suppose it's a child? Hell, Anya, a full-grown man might come out second-best in a fight with that brute. I don't mind admitting I'm leery of him myself."

"He's not vicious. He's not going to hurt anyone."

Tom made a sound of exasperation. Anya knew then she was holding her own. Tom and Richard could have taken him by force; she couldn't have stopped them. But he was still trying to convince her, which meant she had a chance, Casey had a chance.

Richard's eyes said sorrowfully this was betrayal. In a way it was true but Richard's life wasn't in danger. She refused to believe that.

Casey had no one else.

Her legs trembled, her hands and arms ached but it was Tom and Richard who turned away, finally. With another accusing look, Richard murmured something about walking Tom to his car. They hadn't given up; they were only retiring from the field to plot new strategy. She almost smiled but caught herself as Tom turned back to point a finger.

"You let him loose once," he threatened, "just once without a leash and I will hunt him down and I will shoot him where he stands."

Casey's body filled out, his wounds healed as quickly as the quilt took shape in her hands. She watched him pace, his eyes bright, his coat shiny, muscles sliding under his skin; the sight was so beautiful her breath caught in her throat. Here was health and strength, things she had never truly appreciated when she still had them.

Richard and the dog tolerated each other. Though he said no more about turning Casey over to Tom — biding his time — his silences could have been no colder if she had taken a lover.

Anya had to walk Casey. She couldn't ask Richard to do it and even Elizabeth was afraid of him. The first time, she thought he would get the leash tangled around her canes, jerk her off her feet, but it never happened. With almost human understanding, he took the role of protector, not only careful in his own movements but alert to other dangers.

Once when they were walking, a toad popped out of the grass near her feet. Instantly, Casey leaped to stand between her and the small brown thing, hackles rising, a fearsome growl coming from his throat. The toad disappeared. Laughing, she knelt to throw her arms around the dog.

He stayed beside her in the shop. The tourists who came to look at quilts or wall hangings kept their distance but their children knew what they did not. They patted his head, climbed on his back, pulled his tail. Casey enjoyed the attention, though he never willingly left her side.

When the silk patchwork was assembled she was reluctant to begin quilting; she didn't want to finish, to risk having to sell it. For over a week she left it rolled up.

Richard had gone to Asheville and wouldn't be back until late. He hadn't said why he was going. He said less and less these days.

Anya wandered through the house, dusting haphazardly, trying to deny her unease. Casey's toenails clicked behind her as she went from room to room. The heat wave had broken weeks before but tonight the air was heavy. Hoping for a breeze she opened the side window, the one she usually kept closed because it was unscreened and had a low sill. It didn't occur to her there was any risk. Casey was so obedient, sensing what she wanted even when she didn't speak.

With one brief, apologetic look he leaped over the sill and was gone.

She dropped her canes to lean out, calling in an urgent whisper, afraid to raise her voice. Someone might be passing, someone who would report to Tom. Casey bounded through the yard, over the fence. For a moment she could not move. Tom. His threat. Her own weakness. She was alone with this and helpless.

Something called to her, a whispered promise.

Awkwardly, struggling with her canes and the slippery silk, she carried the top, now basted to batting and lining, to the quilting frame. She hadn't stenciled in the pattern. The light was weak. But she had to keep busy or she would go mad with worry. Her ears strained to detect the sound of a shot.

He bounded through the field, reveling in the scents. There was joy in movement, the ripple of muscles, the freedom. His ears pricked to the smallest sounds, a rabbit darting through the grass, hiss of tires on the road below, a distant voice. Nothing fettered him, not walls, nor the leash, nor the woman.

Sitting in the closed-up shop, stitching, she tried to imagine where he was, what he was doing. With her whole being she wished him safe. Like a sorceress crouching over a bowl of water she felt/heard/scented all that he might be experiencing. It brought a rush of remembrance: lights and heat, a body moving in a pattern, the thrill of being truly alive. This was the thing he'd been created for. He needed freedom to the same degree he needed air — as she did, though she had denied it.

Light glistened on the needle as it licked in and out of the fabric.

He lifted his head. With a bark of delight he dashed to the left, ignoring the rhododendrons that brushed his coat. He stopped again where the land dropped away. The sound of panting was loud. One scent, one in particular, created in him a long-unfelt tingling tightness.

The needle rose like a blind thing from the other side. Anya knew where she was, what she did, but the other scene was more real to her than any she had lived, except in the places, lost to her now, where life was distilled to its essence.

Picturing what might lie before the dog's eyes, she recognized the sagging barn, the ramshackle house half-hidden by the barn, the rusting blue Chevy. She had seen this before but from another perspective, a car parked in the yard when she came to buy eggs. A stoop-shouldered farmer came from the barn, fastened the door with a length of wire. Billy Vance, perpetually sour, scowling.

The smell thickened, making Casey quiver.

Vance walked to the house. Desire drew the dog, slinking and wary, down the slope. There was the clack of a screen door.

Behind the weathered gray siding, the object of Casey's attention was yipping softly as if she sensed the need for quiet. The urge was so strong Anya couldn't keep her thoughts separate — if they ever had been, as if this was happening anywhere but in her own mind. A hunger she had not felt for over a year made her ache.

Casey sniffed the lower edge, found a weakness and began to scrabble. Dirt and splinters flew. His former wariness was forgotten. He knew nothing but

need and the intoxicating scent.

The needle was hot. Once more it plunged and then the tingle became a smothering wave. Her hips jerked, twice, unstoppably. The movement brought no release. She leaned forward, clutched the quilting frame, aware of the darkness beyond the windows, the light illuminating her as if she were on a stage. Exposed. Her shame was one with the punishing pain. It was a long moment before the spasm released her and she could raise her head.

Hours later she heard a soft thud, the click of toenails. She pulled herself from bed, hurried to close the window. His eyes laughed in the lamplight; his tongue lolled. She got out a rag to wipe the dirt from his coat before Richard returned, before he could see and guess what she had done — allowed.

It would never happen again, she promised herself.

He saw her face touched by moonlight, lines of pain erased by that magic light. He wanted to kiss her awake, to talk, to remove the shadow that had grown between them. But when he went to her he found Casey on the floor between their beds. The dog gave him a look that might have been contempt or warning. Richard turned away.

In the morning it all seemed foolish. She was cheerful, buoyantly so, and carried Richard along with her mood. At breakfast they talked as if nothing had ever been wrong. Leaving, he tossed a comment over his shoulder, something about seeing if Elizabeth could take care of the shop so they could get away. He didn't notice her fading smile.

When the car was out of sight, she hurried into the shop, giving in to a longing she'd felt the moment she opened her eyes. She slowed when she came near the frame. Nearly a third of the design had been filled in.

They did not go away that week-end. Richard took a hard look at their bank balance, noted that a payment was due on the loan, and said they would have to put off their holiday. Unless, he said, smiling, she sold a quilt.

Anya feigned disappointment, feeling like a traitor. She didn't want to leave Casey.

The next afternoon, Friday, something happened that made her forget her own problems. A party of tourists had just come in when Elizabeth's father appeared, his face sweaty, unshaven. He threatened the girl, his words obscene. Elizabeth cowered; the tourists fled. Anya levered herself from her chair. In fumbling for her canes she dropped one. As she groped for it she shouted at him to leave Elizabeth alone. Fear thinned her voice, made her sound like a weak old woman.

"Stay out of this! This is all your fault — don't think I don't know it — teaching her to paint herself like a slut —" He pulled things from his pockets, lipsticks, brushes, small bottles.

From nowhere it seemed, because he was so well-behaved in the shop she almost forgot him, Casey leaped, snarling like something from a nightmare. It happened so fast Anya couldn't tell whether he actually bit the man or whether he simply put on a show. She made no attempt to call him off. Shaking with rage, she felt like an animal herself; she wanted to howl, wanted the satisfaction of ripping flesh.

Crashing into displays, kicking uselessly at that snarling mass of muscle and teeth, he escaped, stopping in the yard to scream threats. But with Casey braced in the doorway, hackles raised and fangs showing, he wouldn't dare come back.

Anya held Elizabeth while she cried and between fits of sobbing the story came out. It wasn't just the make-up,

though that was bad enough in the eyes of someone with his rigid beliefs — beliefs that didn't preclude taking her pay to spend on booze, Anya commented to herself. Elizabeth had been sneaking out to see someone, waiting until her father was too drunk to know what she was doing. He'd found out somehow; someone must have seen them. His quarrel with her had started at breakfast. She showed Anya the bruises, swollen and purple.

No point in keeping the shop open now. Anya took Elizabeth into the house.

It was near sunset when Elizabeth's grandmother arrived.

Richard's secretary claimed he was in his office with a client but he didn't return her phone calls. Any other time Anya might have entertained jealous fears; now she had no time. She hadn't dared phone Tom to ask what could be done to protect the girl. She would have had to tell him what Casey had done. With the ugly scene fresh in her mind she mistrusted all men. Elizabeth insisted she must go home, face her father, get the punishment over with or it would be worse when he caught her. Her grandmother arrived before she had found the courage to leave but the sick, fearful look in the woman's eyes warned Anya there would be little help from her.

"I can take her in for the night," she said. "But it won't do any good. She's his daughter. She's got to go back. She shouldn't have made him so mad."

Anya's pleading came to nothing. They thought it was right for a man to beat a disobedient child, beat her senseless, if he chose. Grandmother scoffed at Elizabeth's bruises, implying they were nothing compared to what she'd suffered herself. Anya mentioned shelters, counselling, legal protection. She might have been speaking a foreign language. Such things, they said, would only make him more angry; he would find the girl wherever she was hiding and he would kill her, as well as anyone who tried to interfere.

When they left, Anya stumped through the house, wanting to strike out at the walls, the furniture, but the thought of even these small acts of violence frightened her. She hated all men, despised her own weakness. Such brutality should be stopped and all she had offered was words. How was she different from Elizabeth and her grandmother, passively accepting this as if it had been decreed by God?

But what if they were right? What if her interference finally tipped that man over the edge?

She wanted Richard, wanted him now. She needed to talk, to be with him.

He phoned to say he would be late, no explanation for it or for his earlier failure to return her calls. She didn't mention what had happened. Her hands trembled as she put down the phone.

Blood thoughts. Ghosting through darkness on pads that made no sound. The air was electric with the terror of small things that sensed his presence. Sniffing the air, seeking. Lips wrinkled back in a soundless snarl, saliva dripping. Moon's light, witchlight, turning the night to silver and shadows. Muscles sliding under taut skin, stalking, his steps an ancient choreography. Dancing, to vengeance.

Anya stitched, crouched over the frame like an old woman, unaware what her hands were doing, alive only in her mind. God's Eye. All-seeing.

She lusted for revenge as only the powerless can.

Hours later she straightened. Pain was fire. She felt ancient, a crone poisoned by decades of hatred, sucked dry by the sorcery that was her only strength. She looked at her hands and was almost surprised to find they were not wrinkled, gnarled, liver-spotted. She

was the same. But in spite of pain and self-disgust, she felt cleaner for having indulged in that orgy of imagined vengeance. She was purged of her desire to repay suffering with death.

Elizabeth came to work as usual. Richard slept until noon. They had three customers in the shop all day; none of them made a purchase. Casey licked his paws and stared at nothing, darkly. The quilting pattern was nearly finished.

On Sunday afternoon Tom came to ask what happened in the shop on Friday. He had, apparently, already been told something but he did not mention Casey, nor did Anya. Elizabeth's father was missing; he'd not been seen since late Friday night. Richard waited until the sheriff was gone, then looked at her accusingly.

"When I got home on Friday the side window was open."

"Where were you on Friday?" she countered. His lie was thin and he knew she knew it.

She spent the afternoon cutting pieces, stitching blocks for a new patchwork, pretending to be absorbed in her work. He washed the car, taking twice as long as the job warranted.

Child-like, she wondered if because she had wished for a death she had caused it. Wished fervently. Plotted what she would have done if she'd had Casey's strength, his murderous rage, his powerful jaws.

But that was only dreaming and dreams had no power.

Summer's heat had fled; there was a chill in the air every morning. School started and Elizabeth came to the shop only in the afternoons.

She was staying with her grandmother. Anya could scarcely believe the change in her; her face glowed when she mentioned the boy she was seeing.

Grandmother, she said, had given only grudging approval. The sheriff learned that her father owed someone a great deal of money. Only his mother believed he would be back any time soon.

Anya had taken the silk patchwork from the frame, still unfinished. It would bring a good price and, with little coming in this time of year, Richard was worried about making payments on the loan. But she didn't want to finish it. She didn't want to sell it, lose it.

It seemed sheer bad luck that the very hour when her guilt had compelled her to spread the God's Eye silk on her work table to make plans for finishing and binding it, Richard came into the shop with a stranger, a man he introduced as Ben Geller.

"He's going to be our neighbor, just signed the papers for that white house down the road."

"I always liked that house," Anya said. "It has a wonderful view of the valley."

Geller nodded absently, staring at the patchwork.

"This is God's Eye, isn't it? I've never seen that folded thing in the center before. Your own design?"

When he touched it Anya shivered. With growing dread, with growing certainty that it was, in some way, part of a pattern, she heard him say he was a collector. There in Richard's hearing he made an offer that stunned her. He knew what he wanted and was, apparently, wealthy enough to get it. She didn't have to look at Richard to know he was calculating how many loan payments that sum would cover.

He took her to the Vance farm to buy eggs. A dog ambled across the yard, a young bitch, heavily pregnant. Vance cursed the stray that had broken into his barn when she was in heat. She had papers, he said, and he'd wanted to wait until she was older before breeding her.

Anya counted back and felt sick.

Richard looked at her strangely. Of course he didn't mind, he said. The sheriff's office wasn't far out of their way.

But Tom knew no more than before. "I wouldn't worry about Elizabeth if I was you. Likely by the time her daddy gets back she'll have a husband and a baby to show him."

"But she has two years before graduation."

"Girls get married young around here."

He was probably right. They would marry young if the situation at home was like Elizabeth's, and possibly they'd find themselves trapped in the same pattern of violence.

As they were leaving, Tom leaned back in his swivel chair, making it screech. "How's that dog of yours doing?"

"Fine. He's never a bit of trouble."

"Someone said he saw him one night a few weeks back. Out by Henson's. Recognized him as the one from your shop."

Henson's was on the other side of Drover Trail, near the trailer where Elizabeth had lived with her father.

"Must have been another dog," she said. "Casey never goes out without his leash."

Tom nodded, then added softly, "I'd be worried about him if I was you. Some day when you least expect it he might just turn on you."

Richard's silence was chilly.

She cupped Casey's head in her hands, looked into his golden brown eyes. He gazed back trustfully. He doesn't have an ounce of meanness in him, she thought, remembering how gentle he was with children. But I do. She thought about possession, still wanting to believe imagination had no power. She thought about God's Eye.

She would have to finish it soon. Richard had mentioned the loan payment coming due.

She had to know. But what would it prove?

Richard was out for the evening, meeting with someone about a will. When leaving he'd made a wide detour around Casey, sprawled on the rug. He still disliked and mistrusted the dog. The feeling was mutual.

When she came back from the porch, Casey was waiting at the window. It made her wonder how he always knew what she was thinking. For a time she stared into his eyes until she could see nothing else. Finally she forced herself to look away, her eyes tearing. She went to the window and thumbed the catch.

"This is the last time. The very last time."

His muscles tensed. He sprang and was gone.

The needle slid in and out of the silk. Touched with fire from the overhead light, the sight dazzled her, made her lose all sense of her surroundings.

Racing through darkness. The elastic feel of healthy muscles being used as they were meant to be. Head up, scenting, questing. Blood thoughts. Remembering. In her waking dream, their thoughts and souls were one.

As before he avoided roads, bounding through fields and stands of fragrant pine, pausing in clearings to sniff, to listen before hurrying on. No hate this night, only urgency. By scent alone s/he followed the path below the road, the tunnel roofed with pine, walled with brush, behind the trailer. The path known only to the man who had walked it, night after night. If it existed, but of course it did not. Thoughts were tangled, not as they had been before. There was no joy tonight. Discovering the expected scent, dark and unpleasant.

Someone shook her violently. Richard, his face strangely both pale and shadowed.

"What's wrong? Are you sick?"

"I didn't hear you come in."

"Damn right you didn't," he said, straightening. "I've been shaking you for five minutes."

He helped her to her feet. Her legs were as responsive as wood, but wood aflame with pain. She would not cry out, would not look up because then he would see how bad it was. Instead she looked at the pattern of quilting stitches. It was complete, every tiny white thread part of a swirl that drew the eye to the center of God's Eye. What did it mean, now that it was finished?

Tonight s/he had found what she hoped/dreaded to find because she had written the script and painted the scenery. It meant nothing.

"What? What did you say?"

He eased her into the chair next to the side window, now closed. Casey ambled from the bedroom, yawning and stretching as if he had been there all evening.

"I said Elizabeth's father won't hurt her again. Some boys found his body in a hollow about a quarter of a mile from their trailer. As soon as I heard, I came to tell you."

"How did he die?"

She couldn't avoid looking at Casey. Richard looked also, but incuriously.

"A broken neck."

She felt no relief.

"He must have been drunk. Stumbled on the trail and fell."

Or trying to escape a wrathful horror, an animal possessed, that leaped at him from the darkness. Her mouth was dry. She couldn't ask if Richard had closed the window. Had she opened it? Or had that — too — been imagination?

"That quilt is finished, isn't it?"

She shivered slightly and he seemed to think she had shaken her head.

"I know you don't want to sell it. It's your own design. If money wasn't so

©'Walters

tight now I wouldn't ask. But Geller knows the value of what he's buying. Finish it, Anya. We'll take some of that money and get away for a real vacation. You need it. We need time together, time to talk."

"I just have to do the binding," she said weakly, knowing it would be taken as agreement. She didn't want to leave — to leave Casey.

Had she let him out? Or was that part of her nightmare fantasy?

While Richard stopped to turn out the lights, Anya went to bed. She'd taken something for the pain and her thoughts were fuzzy but she couldn't get comfortable. She twisted this way and that, finally pinpointing the source of her discomfort as a small hardness between the sheets. She pulled out a brown button. Must have fallen off her dress when she was changing the sheets.

She held it to her nose, imagining she smelled something unpleasant. She looked at Casey, lying between the beds as if to make certain Richard would have trouble reaching her for their goodnight kiss. He yawned and dropped his head to the rug.

The morning Ben Geller came to pick up the quilt, their bags were packed, Elizabeth had arrived to take care of Casey, and the car was ready. They only had to stop in town to cash Geller's check.

She'd gone over the arrangements with Elizabeth several times. The girl seemed almost as excited about this as Richard. She promised to walk the dog often and no, she said, she wasn't afraid of him now. The shop would remain closed. Casey's care was more important than another sale.

Finally she couldn't invent another reason for delay.

They drove to the coast, to a motel near the beach. They would, Richard promised, do nothing more than soak up sun, eat too much, and read. And talk. She had brought fabric and thread for a new quilt. Richard sighed when he saw the workbag but he said nothing. To placate him she didn't open it for two days.

But they didn't talk, not really. They each skirted the edges of the thing as if afraid to stick a toe in the water.

The big dog was thirsty. He paced through the shop, whining at the places where the woman usually sat, the familiar smell of the things she handled. He felt shame for having relieved himself here. But worse than shame was the thirst, its torment as bad as anything he had suffered in the other place. He had long since stopped trying the door to the house. There was never a response to his scratching, only sometimes laughter, voices.

Her hands itched for something to do. She waited until Richard went to town to pick up a newspaper, then pulled out the green and white fabric and the pattern for Hunter's Star. It was a relief to work. She was sick with worry and weary of the effort to convince Richard she was having a good time. She became absorbed in the familiar motions of cutting and stitching. It wasn't the same as with God's Eye — though she tried, freeing her mind, concentrating on thoughts of him running free — but of course he wasn't running free.

When the phone rang, she dropped the scissors. It wasn't a wrong number or Richard calling with news from town. She knew.

Tom walked across the graveled lot in front of the shop. Window broken out, just like the neighbor reported. He paused there, guessing what had happened from the fact that shards of glass and pieces of the frame were outside. It was a shame, a damn shame.

The girl's shirt was buttoned wrong.

Alone? Of course she was — but her eyes said she lied — and no, she hadn't heard anything. Tom didn't ask permission and she didn't refuse, not in words, but he bulled his way in like he had a right to be here. The boy was gone. Caught a glimpse of a shirttail when he looked out the back window but no point in chasing him. Both of them needed spanking, not arresting. The dog, he asked.

Wide, innocent eyes. She'd tried, she said, but he wouldn't let her near. She showed him marks on her arm, could have been made by teeth or could have been rough play with the boyfriend.

Anya would be heartbroken. A damn shame. Tom was sorry as Hell about the whole thing.

She found herself holding a completed block, crumpled and sweaty. She smoothed it out, traced the pattern with her finger. Where was he? Tom had offered little hope. He would try to take the dog without hurting him, he said, but he wouldn't risk anyone's safety. Satisfaction in his voice he scarcely tried to conceal. He'd only been waiting for this chance.

Richard's foot was heavy on the accelerator. Anya interpreted his silence as relief and an attempt to spare her feelings. He wouldn't be sorry to find Casey dead when they got back. It made her furious but she couldn't risk a fight now. She needed him.

But she hated them both — all men — hated them.

Thirst slaked and hunger satisfied, the dog felt playful, his ordeal forgotten. Running, breathing deep, muscles strained but not nearly to their limits. Pausing to scent the air he heard a rustle in some brush, wheeled, and started after the rabbit. He nearly ran it down but at the last, when another leap would have brought him near enough to close his jaws around it, he dropped his forepaws to the ground, his rear still sticking up in the air, tail wagging, and he let it get away.

Rising, shaking himself, he trotted on.

Beneath some pines overlooking a road he stopped again. Something in the air. Something sharp, sweetly piercing. He trembled. Whined. Crouched. Shivering constantly now with joy-turned-to-pain, he tried to burrow into the carpet of pine needles. No escape. It came closer.

Another mile, maybe two. Anya gasped.

"You all right?" He took his hand from the wheel, touched hers, lying like a dead thing in her lap.

She still felt the trembling inside. Where — But he was alive; it couldn't have been imagination, wishful thinking. He was alive and she might be in time to save him. If she only knew where. She looked down, found the Hunter's Star in pieces. She'd picked out all the threads.

With a cry, Richard wrenched at the wheel. The car swerved, there was an explosive sound, shuddering, an instant on the edge of loss of control. He stopped the car at the side of the road.

"What's wrong?"

He raised a shaking hand to his head. "Something came at us. Didn't you see? Jumped in front of the car." He fumbled for the door handle.

"We can't stop now!" But he wasn't there to hear. She followed, found him staring at a front tire, nearly shredded.

"Good thing we weren't going any faster. Would have killed us."

Relief in his voice. Oh, yes. Anything to give Tom more time. Fury left her weak — she was always — would always be weak and useless. She clenched her teeth. Her legs were trembling so she had to lean against the car. Rage, blinding her. He'd always resented Casey, resented anyone else coming into her life. He wanted to be the strong one, the protector — the possessor. A cane dropped from her nerveless hand.

He was at the trunk, wrestling with the spare, his face red/black/red/black in the blink of the flashers. A mask, the face of a monster, not someone she knew.

Anya moved toward him. On the ground, shreds of cloth, shapes in green and white.

Where was she?

Running, magic silver light changed to the color of blood, the scent of blood in the air, and joy. A strong, healthy body exulting in freedom, racing through the night.

No.

She stopped, looked down at the tips of her canes on the paving, her useless legs. She was panting for breath and her hands ached from gripping her canes. Where was the car? She recognized the road, knew she was about a mile from their house but where was Richard? Why was she here, alone?

Blood. The scent of it in the air, the slick feel of it on her hands. An image of Richard, falling, a look of terror on his face, red/black/red/black.

Her cry was an animal sound. What was happening? What had she done?

Once more she lost herself, lost the pain that fettered her, lost the weakness that shackled her to the life of an invalid, dependent on the strength of others. Once more she ran free on strong legs, her healthy body racing for the sheer joy of it. Scorn for those who feared her, those men who would stop her, kill her if they could.

A blink, a cry. She slipped into pain as fingers would slip into a glove. Was she losing her self, her soul? Was it sorcery or only insanity?

Only. She laughed, a ragged sound. Her husband dead or dying on the road and when they found her, the blood on her hands, they would decide she was only insane. They would lock her in a prison. But she knew about prisons; her body was one. Only. Insane.

She stumped along the road, slowed by her useless legs, trapped in nightmare. Where was she going?

She knew when she saw the house set back from the road. Geller's house. The quilt, the God's Eye patchwork. That was the pattern that had called him to her, trapped them in the center of God's Eye.

Gravel spewed as Richard wrenched at the wheel and jammed on the brakes. The house was dark. Blood dripped into his eyes from the gash in his head; he rubbed it away, stabbed the house key into the lock, nearly broke down the door when it didn't unlatch the first time. Common sense was telling him — he wasn't listening — that if the house was dark, the door still locked, she wasn't here. He went from room to room, turning on lights, shouting her name. She had to be here. Where else? Why had she left him after he fell, scraping his head on the jack? Had she gone for help?

That Goddamn dog. Jumping on them like that. Of course he was glad to see her. She was his angel, his protector. Casey's devotion to Anya was the only reason Richard tolerated him. Couldn't take that from her, that happiness, after she'd lost, suffered so much. But he'd never jumped at her like that before. What had gotten into him tonight?

Richard slumped in a chair, her chair, not knowing what to do. He'd lost consciousness for a minute or two, which had to be why he was confused now. Tom. The sheriff. Of course. He reached for the phone and it shrilled, like a terrified animal expecting a blow from his raised hand.

Lights blazed from Geller's house and from the light bar on the sheriff's car, clicking, turning. The door was open. They were waiting for him, Tom and Ben Geller, not speaking, not going near her.

She looked a thousand years old, her legs asprawl, hair tangled, hands lying beside her as if they didn't belong to her. On the floor, shreds of colored silk. She didn't look up, didn't respond to their presence. Staring at nothing as if her mind was gone. Richard couldn't speak.

The silk, like a drift of autumn leaves: golden brown, sable, orange, emerald green. It looked as though at first she had tried to pick them apart and then, giving in to impatience, ripped at them with her teeth. There was a thread hanging from her mouth.

No one moved or spoke.

Click of toenails. Casey looking up with an expression that could only be laughter. Whining, gazing adoringly at him, ignoring Anya. His tail, his whole rear end, wagging. With a yip the dog rose on his hind legs, braced his paws on Richard's shoulders, licked his face. Richard, shocked, pulled away.

A bark, a playful crouch, then a leap out the door, into the night.

Movement. Darkness and light. Colors whirled and streamed in patterns that formed, broke, reformed, as in a kaleidoscope. Rays and arrows of color as if from a blazing eye, God's Eye. Anya never again dreamed of dancing.   Ω

FRIDAY NIGHT!

Friday night is Fright Night!
And things that haven't breathed
In ages . . . still seek *something* . . .

Some gliding, some walking,
Some stumbling about
Like the blind, or drunken fools —
And all carry with them
Truly ominous tools.

Butcher knives, cleavers,
Chains — axes, too —
Oh, important things these are,
If members of this Friday group
Seek to sup beneath the stars.

Now comes deathsilence
As you they surround,
With all their stench and doom.
You look where their eyes should be —
But behold only gloom.

Yes! Friday night is Fright Night!
And they'll feel no hunger here:
They'll feast upon your cries and
    screams
And drink up all your fears!

— **Lynne Armstrong-Jones**

107

LUNCH WITH MOTHER

by James Irving Ross

"Some space, mother. That's all I wanted. Just a little space."

"What you wanted, Virgil, was to leave me to rot."

"We certainly don't have to worry about that now, do we?"

"I should have known you were planning to run out. Just like old jellyknees."

"Cut the crap, mother. Your badgering's what sent pop down the road."

"Ha! How would you know? You were only seven years old."

"Let it rest."

"You remind me of him more all the time. Like now. How many times have you been told to sit up straight at the table?"

"Drop it, mother."

"He was a snivelling simp. Anyway, like I said this morning, I only told her for your own good. Yours *and* hers. It wasn't just to keep you here. I was sure you'd understand."

"Understand? Oh, I understand clearly. I understand that for thirty-one years I've been suffocating in this dilapidated, washed-out nook of a town that barely rates a dot on a map. For thirty-one years I've lived in this creaky, Leave-It-To-Beaver, two-story house, constantly cringing under the glare of your steely eyes. And all along you've kept me strapped to your merry-go-round of guilt, squeezing me to the point where I couldn't even dream of finding the courage to drop out of your sadistic little parade and have a life."

"Nonsense! We've been over it and over it, Virgil. A son's first responsibility is to his mother. Particularly when she gets old and decrepit."

"You're fifty-seven and sturdy enough to split a cord of hickory without rest. I've seen you do it. So you can save the horseshit sympathy routine for some other gullible moron."

"Don't you dare be cross with *me,* boy. I need you here and that's all there is to it. Case closed. Now shut your filthy mouth and eat. Otherwise —"

"Otherwise what? I'll spend a week in the shed? Don't you see, mother? You can't punish me any more. That's what this specially prepared lunch is all about. We're celebrating my emancipation. That's why I did it. To be free. Isn't it obvious?"

"You've gone totally insane, that's why you did it. And all because I told Holly the truth and kept her from making a grievous mistake."

"We loved each other."

"She had to be told about your *perversion,* Virgil. And that you talk to yourself. There was no getting around it. No sir. It was only right that she know the reasons you'll never do better than hacking chickens apart at Skinner's poultry farm — that you've been mentally disturbed ever since —"

"Please, mother."

"Ever since you did those *things* to that Casey girl."

"Couldn't let it pass, could you? How many times have you waved it in my face, and how many times have I explained? I was nineteen and crazy scared. I pled guilty because you made me. It was a pure case of mistaken identification, *and you know it.*"

"Says you. And don't make it sound so simple. There was restitution, legal expenses, and a watchful eye to be kept on that girl's father for quite a time. Thought I'd never wangle you out of that one."

"You're preaching on Bad Boy Virgil again, mother."

"You had a bent mind then and still do. What you've just done speaks for itself. End of sermon. Happy?"

"A sick mind. Crazy. A lunatic. That's all I've ever heard. Occasional kind words or a longer leash might have changed everything. But no."

"You'll never justify it that way."

"There was no other solution. That's justification enough."

"You're gonna have to do better than that, sick-o."

"You don't get it, do you?"

"The police won't get it, that's for sure. And they're probably on their way now. The postman passed by a minute ago and glanced in the window. I saw his eyes bug and the color jump right out of his face. He left in a stumbling run."

"Doesn't matter."

"Such a mess, Virgil. Your clothes, the tablecloth . . ."

"I have scored a great victory, one that can never be changed or undone. No matter what else happens, I'll bask in that sunshine from now on. I've won, mother. I've won."

"I hear a siren, Virgil. Are you just going to sit there?"

"Not at all, mother dear. I'm going to finish what's on my plate . . . like you always say."

"Then at least wipe the blood from your chin and sit up straight.

"And for God's sake, son, stop talking to yourself."

Ω

A GOURMAND
OF THE MUTANT RAIN FOREST

His jaded palate
is startled and refreshed
by a wealth of flavors
so subtle and provocative
that frissons of delight
shudder up and down
his meaty back,
by pungent aromatics
so utterly unique
he once again discovers
the first unbounded passion
of his sensual decay.

From a penthouse suite
safe within the Seattle dome,
he expends his fortune
on delicacies more
bizarre and illicit
than a cannibal's feast.
He bribes customs officials
and employs unsavory sorts
so that he might savor
the fruits and meats
of a furious ecology,
so that his tastebuds
might embark upon
vicarious exploration
of far rivers and climes
he would never dare
to visit in the flesh.

Even the pains which
rack his portly belly
do not lessen his desire
for spiny bone white guavas
seasoned with banana moss.
The rash of radiation welts
which erupts upon his chest,
his throat and forearms,
does not delay his hunt
for the perfect table red
to complement the spicy
roasted sweetbreads
of the anaconda sloth.

He is discovered
one morning slumped
before his laden table,
nearly unrecognizable
in the stench of his decay.
The slender stalks
of saffron fungi
which sprout
from all his orifices
have reduced him
to an ectomorph
and scoured
the plates before him
till they shine,
yet have left
a ghastly rictus
of gluttony revered
upon his face.

— **Bruce Boston**

SPEARS OF
THE SEA-WOLVES

by Keith Taylor

"Gwlythin! What is it?"

The girl's voice trembled, and hearing it quiver she drew three careful breaths to bring it within her own command again. Standing upon the neglected battlements of a fortress high above the sea with the briny wind in her hair, she looked very much alone; a woman-child of fifteen with the puppy-softness of that age, skin fine as an infant's, and eyes of surpassing clarity. Those grey orbs had already looked upon things few women ever saw, but they had the innocence of a new-born lamb's to the eyes of the one she addressed as Gwlythin. •

Her teacher never moved. Standing at the very edge of the rampart, she stared in a black trance at the waves below, marking their pattern as they crashed and withdrew. Once the sea had kept a respectful distance from the foundations of this fort, as the pirate Saxons and Jutes had shown a wary respect for the civilized fleet that patrolled the channel. Once. Now the surf boomed hollowly at the base of the very wall, hurling fans of spray so high that tiny droplets moistened Gwlythin's snowy hair.

Although white at three-and-forty, she was not frail. The lines cut deeply into her face had been incised more by her own harsh character than by time. Gwlythin's bones remained strong; not one tooth was missing from her head. The peasants whispered in malice and fear that she had been born with them all, the mark of a shape-changer. Gwlythin neither denied nor admitted such rumors.

Her dark eyes studied the sea from between narrowed lids as its waves gathered, crashed, and peeled back from the shore in foam. To her they conveyed messages in subtle writing. The girl behind her did not speak again, and in her own time Gwlythin turned around, her face bleak with despair. She had deciphered news in the breaking waves; tidings from across the sea and from inland Britain, carried down by rivers stained crimson.

"What has the wind told you?" she demanded.

"Nothing." The girl sounded defensive. "It blows from the east."

Gwlythin snorted. "A paltry excuse! You haven't yet learned to understand it well enough. Vivayn, it doesn't help to be naturally gifted if you will not exercise your gifts, and certain it is you have none at all for water sorcery. I'd make you divine the news I have by your own powers, if I had time, but there is none."

"Say it to me." Vivayn had turned pale to the lips.

"Your sire received no help, from the Summer Country or the Atrebates. Instead of fleeing, he chose to meet Cerdic with the forces he could raise alone. That accursed sea-wolf broke them in an hour. It's grief unto me that I say this, girl, but he has slain the king. Hamo is completely fallen now."

Slain the king. Slain my sire. The words tolled and rang uselessly in Vivayn's head, bearing a freight of meaning she was not yet ready to accept. Hamo fallen, taken by the heathen sea-wolves as Kent had been taken, like all the other lands of the Saxon Shore, whose name had become literal truth. Her father lay dead, dead, butchered by stinking savages with lice in their beards!

She could not believe it. No, not even though the devil called Cerdic had encamped on an island off her father's coast for years, laughing at British attempts to dislodge him, growing ever richer and stronger, taking tribute even from Vivayn's father in the final years. It had been inevitable that one day he would lead his monsters to the mainland and pillage Hamo on the estuary, yet foolishly they had all behaved as though that day would never come. Thus it had taken them by surprise, so that the smoke of the burning town still clung to Vivayn's cloak and bronze-red hair. Like her father, she had escaped that first onslaught of Cerdic's barbarians, and believed that with his neighbor kings' help he would still throw them back into the sea they defiled. Now — it couldn't be!

"It can be." Gwlythin read her mind, or perhaps the movement of her pale lips. "It is. More than that, the ship which should have taken you all to safety in this misfortune will not come. It met some of Cerdic's wolves, hastening late to the feast. Say a prayer for some brave men's souls, Vivayn, then think of what you will do. Deeply as those Jutish hogs fear all Rome's works, they will come searching this fort eventually, and you must not be here."

A note of finality in the older woman's voice reached Vivayn. She said, "I hear only *you,* and nothing of *us.* We're all departing together, my teacher, aren't we?"

Gwlythin smiled more gently than her custom was, which frightened Vivayn more in the circumstances than if she had snapped a rebuff. "No. Listen, child, who cannot be a child forever, I'm an aged woman. The sea-wolves will simply cut my throat if they catch me anyhow. You were born for a greater and better fate than that. Besides, you're young. Life still holds things for you. I have seen those beasts conquer more and more of Britain while our own kings, your father among them, did nothing but bicker among themselves. He wasn't altogether blameless that he found himself without friends at the last. Oh, keep his memory dear as a daughter should, but never lose sight of the truth as clearly as you can see it. That is all we have."

"But what of you?" Vivayn burst out.

"I'm taking my own path," Gwlythin answered, still with that gentleness which was so chillingly unlike her. "You must follow yours. If you are wise it will lead to the western mountains, or to the north where your ancestors dwelt and where no sea-wolves have yet landed — and it were best that you went quickly. Now farewell, Vivayn."

Upon that word, and with a determined face, Gwlythin stepped backwards from the rampart. For an instant she seemed to hang poised in the air; then she was gone, hurtling towards the waves whose voices she understood so well, the wind howling about her. Striking the wall and rebounding outwards, Vivayn's teacher was swallowed by the sea. A wild, choked scream marked her passing, not her own but Vivayn's — and when the girl comprehended fully what had happened, she screamed again, more loudly, a long cry of anguish.

Gwlythin! How could you do that? How could you leave me?

Gone in an instant, gone, after telling her that her father, too, was dead and her home irretrievably lost! Gwlythin's discipline, authority, realism had gone with her, the qualities a little band would need most if it was to reach any kind of safety through the plundered countryside. It seemed to Vivayn that those qualities must have been illusions of smoke if Gwlythin could plunge so indifferently to her death, leaving them all to cope without her. No girl of fifteen could lead people desperate for refuge in a world that offered none — save that she was King Natanleod's daughter and they would expect it.

Oh, Gwlythin . . .

Vivayn did not know how long she stood gazing at the wave-surge where her teacher in sorcery had vanished. It must have been longer than she supposed, because a sound of heavy footsteps and panting on the stair to the ramparts made her turn, and she knew how long it took to perform that climb.

"My lady, what happened? I heard that scream, and then naught!"

Vivayn faced the burly, black-haired warrior with the raven brand on his forehead, bracing herself to show no weakness before a man she had never fully liked or trusted. "It was Gwlythin, Junius. She — threw herself into the sea in despair." The truth of that would strike home before long, Vivayn knew. Uttering the words brought it closer. "The sea-waves gave her tidings she could not bear. We had better go down to the others. Now. They must hear."

"The old hag suicided? Blessed Bran! I'd as soon expect that of a crow!" Seeing Vivayn's anger, he shrugged and said falsely, "Sorry, my lady. Sa! It was a long climb for this! We'll go down, then, but I'd rest first."

"No, Junius, this will not wait, alas. We can both rest in the parade yard."

Vivayn moved towards the stair which led into a deep black well, her whole manner taking it for granted that the warrior would step aside for her, then follow to light her way with the crackling torch he carried. To her relief, he did. Something in his murky eyes made her think he had half-conceived the notion of seducing her there on the ramparts. If he found the resolution to attempt it, there was too real a chance that in resisting, Vivayn would go where Gwlythin had gone. She took care to hold her head royally high down all the flights of stone stairs descending the tower. Her father's own man! Far from the best of them, true, or he would have been with him, fighting the invaders, but still — her father's man. How would he be when he learned that King Natanleod lay dead? Safety, protection, privilege, obedience had all disappeared like dew in the morning.

Perhaps some would not understand it so quickly. Vivayn was the kingdom's heiress, and whether or not that still meant anything she could use it to take command. Passing through a tiny, long disused guard-room at the base of the tower to emerge flushed and swift-breathing in the parade yard of the fortress, Vivayn saw the tiny band of refugees who were its sole inhabitants now. Four armed men and one woman rose to greet her, while Junius came lumbering after his king's daughter to douse the half-burnt torch in a barrel and stand winded. He liked work too little and mead too much, else he would never have been shamed in his physical condition by Vivayn.

"My lady," said one of the men. He paused then, struck by the princess's look. Tall, fine-boned, her hair tumbling wild around a delicate oval of a face not yet mature or committed enough to show the kind of woman she would be, Vivayn yet looked sufficiently grave and sorrowful now for a matriarch of fratricidal sons. She walked slowly to the camp-fire they had built in that long-deserted yard where grass grew between the stones.

"I bring heavy news," Vivayn said, her voice bloodless as crystal. "Gwlythin slew herself once she had told it to me, so I must think she knew it true . . . my father was abandoned to face Cerdic with only the few warriors he had. None helped him. Now they are all slain, and Cerdic holds the land as far as Venta uncontested."

The other woman, a servant some ten years older than Vivayn, gave a long vibrating wail and drew a shawl over her head and face. Sinking to her haunches, she rocked back and forth, keening.

"Be silent, Enid!" Vivayn spoke sharply, as Gwlythin might have done, knowing that if she listened to another's grief or envisioned her father's face, she too would shatter in mourning, leaving the leadership to Junius. They could not afford that.

The woman Enid threw back her veil to goggle in outrage at Vivayn, seeing her tearless eyes and calm face as proof that she had no heart. Some of the men's faces registered shock and dawning condemnation also, though one looked approving and the youngest merely crossed himself, then waited to hear more. His name was Cadaran;

Vivayn knew him slightly.

"I've other bad news," she said. "The ship which was to take us to Cornwall has been destroyed by sea-wolves — Jutes or another breed, it matters little. To reach safety we must go by boat through the marsh."

"Our ship gone?" Junius bellowed. "No, by the nine waves of the sea! You lie — I mean the other witch lied! We can't be trapped here! To dare the marsh is to give our heads to death! Are you all going to listen to —"

"To whom, Junius?" Vivayn asked. Now her voice carried a note like splintering ice in the depths of a glacier, fissured with crevasses to swallow the unwary. This was the magic of air for which she had a native talent, with controlling and throwing out tone as one of its earliest, simplest uses. Such razored iciness from her lips made the big man blink and consider.

"— to — a woman young — and without experience of war," Junius said, retreating. "The whole land will be covered with stragglers or followers, hungry for loot. If they come upon us in numbers, they'll slay us or take us for slaves — and what they'll do to the women —"

"You'd know," said the man who had looked approving when Vivayn silenced Enid's wails. Dark, middle-sized and well-built, he had a thin nose and a suggestion of grim drollery in the shape of his mouth. "You'd know, indeed, and even the rest of us can guess. It's a thing that does not need saying aloud. Lady, I wouldn't appear to doubt, but are you certain of what you say?"

"She was certain," Vivayn answered with a little shiver which made her cloak ripple in numerous shades of blue. "Plunging from the battlements would be a fearsome way to convince me of a lie."

"Supposing she's truly dead," Junius said, a contentious twist to his mouth. "Witches can fool even the dark angel."

Anger crackled along Vivayn's overstretched nerves. How dared this oaf denigrate Gwlythin's suicide, doubt that it was real? She concentrated, summoning the powers of illusion she had mastered, wishing she could raise a wind with it, to whip through the yard with a smell of briny dampness.

What she did create proved sufficient. A harsh voice rang off the stone walls, seeming to originate everywhere, a voice they all knew. Junius looked wildly around when he heard it, sudden ludicrous fear in his face.

"Death cannot be fooled, you poor lump of unleavened bread! Turn and look upon me!"

With a stiff face, he did so, and beheld a specter with sea-drenched white hair facing him in the gateway. Her gown dripped, one arm hung limp from the cruel impacts of her fall, and she stared at him with a face paler than her hair.

"You see that I am dead," the illusion said in its chill voice. "Now I speak with sure knowledge and what I say is the truth. Lifeless equally are King Natanleod and all those who fought with him, save what few managed to flee. My lady's life is in your hands and she shall lead you to safety; she alone. Else you shall die like the lustful pig you are. Listen well! A ghost has prophesied for you."

The vision raised its sound arm to point a finger dramatically. Junius stepped back in terror; he had never been brave, despite his size and his gory boasts of all he achieved in battle. In the next moment the specter dissolved in a cloud of sea-mist, and when Junius walked hesitantly to examine the spot where it had addressed him, not a trace of water moistened the stones where its robe had spilled rivulets. Junius knelt before Vivayn with awe in his brutish face.

"Pardon me, lady! Pardon me! It wasn't you I doubted, but Gwlythin! I'm your man now for any endeavor!"

"Then swear that to me upon your life," Vivayn ordered, taking advantage of his fear-inspired fervor before it departed. Junius took her hand between his weapon-hardened palms and swore the oath in a moment. His alacrity was not the most comforting thing in the world; he might forget the oath with equal suddenness at some time in the future, but she had gained his untrustworthy support for the moment.

"Now, good folk, we had better plan our course," Vivayn said.

While they looked at her with doubt, respect, and calculation, according to their natures, Vivayn felt an inner pang of remorse. She had used her teacher's death to cement authority over this band through a cheap trick of illusion, and announced her father's death as a fact through the illusion's lips. She didn't know it for certain. Oaf though he might be, Junius had been right in that at least. Even Vivayn's grim instructress could have been mistaken. A little hope stirred in the girl. Perhaps, just perhaps, her father still lived.

They began to talk. Junius, though he blustered a good deal, showed hard survival sense, and the shortly-spoken man with the thin nose combined the same quality with wits. Enid had no idea of what to do, nor, really, had the admiring youngster who supported Vivayn. He'd be loyal, surely, but he would neither produce ideas nor take initiative.

It lies with me. I tricked my way to leadership, and now I am responsible for these six lives.

Having listened and weighed the information, Vivayn spoke in her natural clear voice, with no tricks of sorcery.

"We cannot leave this place by sea. We've only a little marsh-boat that barely holds us all, and none here is skilled at sailing anyhow. We'd blunder about, and be caught by some Jutish band. Therefore we must go through the marsh, and Hol is the man to guide us."

The smallest of her warriors, an oddly tattooed fellow with the face of a scrofulous gnome, winked confidently in response. They were listening to her, she saw with relief. But what now? All she knew of the countryside came from maps. Wait; there was something more.

"Once through the marsh we will be in a conquered land. Our best hope then is that, as Gwlythin said to me, the sea-wolves fear everything built by Rome. The great stones which walked into place at the bidding of Rome's sorcerers prove that the Jutish gods are meaner than ours. Let us reach Venta, that great abandoned city, and we can hide safely within its walls, then travel north on the highway by night. No Jute would molest us there."

"And how do we reach it unseen?" Junius asked, less belligerently than before. "From here to Venta is a long way."

"I've hunted all across this land in better days," the thin-nosed man said with a reminiscent smile. His name was Keir, and Vivayn knew less about him than about any of the others. "There are tricks I know, and the sea-wolves are blundering strangers. We have a chance. One can't ask more of any god, ours or theirs."

"I too have tricks," Vivayn said. "If enemies come near us, my magic will confuse them, but since it is only powerful at night we had better hide and rest by day."

"Not in the marsh," Hol said abruptly. "Too many evil things moving at night, worse than the Jutes. We find a safe place before sundown and stay there."

From that position they could not budge him, and since Hol was needed indispensably to guide them through the marsh, Vivayn agreed. They boarded the flat-bottomed craft which had brought them to the fort from the blazing town of Hamo, and were poling through the surrounding fen before the sun had moved a hand's width more in the sky. Having little to do but sit in the rear of the punt and think, Vivayn was instantly haunted by visions of a reddened battle-field where savages in wolfskins laughed over their victory and a red-haired king lay grotesque in death with none to straighten his limbs or say a prayer above his bier. She had never been close to her father Natanleod; his main contribution to her upbringing had been to curse the fact that she had no brothers, and leave her alone to cultivate the friendship of the many fortune-tellers, wizards, and other charlatans who passed through his hall. That at least had taught Vivayn to recognize a faker at ten yards' distance — but now the hall where they had congregated lay in burned ashes. Her father was almost surely dead and would never love her now.

Vivayn wanted to weep, yet her heart and eyes alike felt dry. Turning her head away lest tears should come unexpectedly and betray to her companions that she was, after all, only a girl, she watched the clouds reflected in clear water. That surface, sometimes clear, sometimes misted by the breath of the gods, had been the same before the Roman fort had been built, and would be the same still when not three joined stones of it remained.

Behind Vivayn, Enid whispered in outrage to one of the men, "How can she be so cold?"

Because, Vivayn thought, *it is a way to stay untouched by this mad world where Britons fight Britons instead of their common enemy. I envy you, Enid. You can choke and wail a little over the king, and then with your duty done, your feelings relieved, you can bustle along with your life.*

"There," Keir said at last, ceasing to pole. "That island should do. We can rest there tonight and begin again before dawn. What do you say, Hol? My lady? Is it a place of good or bad omen?"

You too? Vivayn thought, sadly

117

amused. *You seem a sensible man, Keir, yet you too believe in omens and luck, and prophecies which nine times in ten are wishful invention. Gwlythin told me that, yet even she could be gullible in that fashion. Yonder place is just an island, with sedges and willows growing green upon it, reflected in water which hasn't a breath of wind to ruffle it. There is a place to hide, as sheltering as any other, and we had no sleep last night. It will do.*

She had learned something, though, from the many fakers who had come to her father's hall. Appearances were important. Having put on a show in the deserted fortress, she must keep it up now, since not only her position but the spirit of this little band could depend on it. Rising gracefully to her feet, she balanced in the rocking boat while gazing at the island, trusting that her manner was duly impressive.

"Yes," she declared, giving her voice the ring of prophecy. "If we pause there we will not be discovered by any evil thing, and we can quit the marshes safely."

They went ashore on her word, and while Keir and Hol hid the boat Enid prepared the last of the food they had brought with them. After they had eaten it, sunset had ended, wherefore Vivayn curled up to sleep on a bed of leaves with a cloak folded under her head. She who had lain on a bed of down nearly every night of her life adapted so well that she scarcely noticed the difference. The turmoil in her heart made a rougher bed than leaves on the ground.

At first Vivayn lay down only because she had to rest in order to stay strong, convinced that her eyes would never close, and for some time she did turn in fidgety torment, images of death in her mind. Finally, though, her body's demands won over her sensitive brain, and she fell into a slumber which — for an hour or two — passed untroubled by dreams. Then they rose to the surface, bubbling and thick; her father, trampled

and hacked apart by men with the faces of beasts; the town of Hamo turned into one screaming bonfire; Gwlythin plunging to her death; and ever recurring, the vision of her father dying on the battlefield, in a different hideous way each time. She moaned, reaching out blindly for comfort, but her fingers found only leaves.

Then it seemed to Vivayn that her teacher stood above her, not broken and drowned but whole, her look one of loving exasperation.

"Little fool," her dream said. "Don't you know that you did well? That lout Junius would have turned them all against you if you hadn't used my ghost to daunt them. The dead deserve no more than tears and the kindest memories of them that we can hold. It's the living who count, always. I abandoned you when I went to my death, and you did what was needful. Never lash yourself for that like some green nun who has had a carnal dream! You did well. Now awaken; there's more to do."

Upon that word, Vivayn blinked and sat up with a suddenness that drew the blood from her tousled head. White as a cloud, she looked into the faces of Enid and Junius, and it seemed to her that the form of her self-slain teacher faded from the air between them as she awoke.

The pair gaped at her. Enid blurted, "My lady! There were visions surrounding you — of the king your father, and Jutish demons, red weapons in a forest — and then it seemed that old Gwlythin came, driving them all away, and spoke to you, whereupon you grew peaceful —"

"It's true," Junius confirmed, with a soberness unlike him. "I'd call it fancy, but I saw it my own self. Aye, and heard."

Those were my very dreams, Vivayn thought confusedly, *and if they both saw it, then Gwlythin's spirit did come! She watches over me!*

"We need your sorcery now," Enid was

saying desperately. "There's a boat, a boat of Jutes coming yonder!"

Jutes! Vivayn's skin grew icy cold. She followed the pair through the bushes, crouching low, until they reached Keir's place of concealment. He greeted them with a terse, "Watch and be quiet," paying no heed to Vivayn's royal rank in that moment. Peering through the leaves of a green willow, Vivayn saw the craft Enid had moaned was coming; no lean, serpent-headed war-boat out of frightened legends, but a shabby brown thing holding no more than twenty men, and they scarcely the giants in horned helmets the stories described. As the boat drew nearer, Vivayn felt almost disappointed that they looked so ordinary.

Not even their leader wore the horned war-hat mandatory to every harper's description. Most, in fact, rowed bareheaded, their grimy hair braided for convenience, though a few did protect their heads with hard leather caps. The only weapons in evidence were spears, stacked amidships in a careful sheaf. The Jutes didn't even look particularly big. They rowed competently, laughed, boasted, and swapped foul jokes in their own language, of which Vivayn understood a good deal. She heard her own name bandied among them as they swept by, which made her furious.

Keir heard it, too. He was familiar with their northern dialect himself. Where and how he had learned it, Vivayn did not know, and this was not a time to ask.

"Sa-ha! No question but that they search for you, lady," Keir said, rubbing his long moustache thoughtfully. "They go to the fortress on their chieftain's orders, to find you; they were bragging of how they would tear it down stone by stone, denying thus their fear of the place. When they do not find you, they'll be back, looking for traces."

"Then let's flee now!" Enid said, and for once, although she did not think of

Enid as bright, Vivayn agreed with her. Keir shook his head.

"We have time. Those dogs must reach the fort, search it, and return. Suppose we panicked now, and ran straight into another boatload of savages following an hour behind them? *Cerdic* has given orders for your capture, lady, and I would guess he offers a reward. We cannot make mistakes."

"It'll be a mistake if we're still here when they come back!" Junius interjected.

"Can your magic help us there, lady?" Keir asked.

"Yes, it can. This is night, and my sorcery is most potent then. Give me till morning, and I'll make this islet invisible to searchers; I mean confuse their eyes with illusion so that they will not see it. That way seems best. It draws no attention."

"You're clever beyond your years," Keir said. He meant it. Most girls of her age, and boys too, would have used such powers as Vivayn's to exaggerated effect, seeking to frighten and impress her enemies — not to mention her friends. The Jutes weren't cowards or fools. If they saw something out of the ordinary, they would investigate it, and they numbered a score.

For a while the fugitives waited in nerve-wracking silence lest another Jutish boat should appear, five men and two women on a piece of ground barely large enough to give them all space to move. No other Jutish craft appeared. Junius opined that it must have stretched even Cerdic's credit as a leader to detach twenty useful men from the merry business of plundering and raping once the battle was over, to travel through a marsh on such a dubious errand.

"One day it'll be their thorps that burn and Jutish women who shriek as strangers grab 'em," he boasted. "Yes, and I'll be there for vengeance!"

"Good," Keir said amiably.

"Yes, they'll learn," Junius repeated

darkly. "When the Household of Britain rides under the dragon banner and the Count's horsemen thunder down Tamesa Valley to the very beaches of Kent, trampling Hengist's brood into the sand, then there'll be payment for all that these boarhogs have done. Natanleod's blood will be avenged like Cain's, my lady — seventy times seven!"

"May we all see it," Keir said, noting the flicker of pain which crossed Vivayn's face, "but for now I'll be content with seeing the other side of this marsh. Lady, I came here a stranger and was well received by your sire; I too will lend my sword to the work of avenging him when the time comes. And it's in your service meanwhile."

"My thanks . . . Keir." Vivayn's voice stumbled a little. The declaration sounded trustworthy, and it moved her, making her feel less terribly alone. "Now I must prepare that sorcery of mine. It's to be cast from the highest place on this little hand-patch of ground, therefore stay at the margin, all of you."

"It's a matter of three yards' distance at most, lady," young Cadaran protested. "Why, if one of us sneezes he'll disturb you."

"That's why we're staying by the water's edge, lad," Keir said. "If you feel a sneeze or a cough impending, just duck your head quietly beneath the surface and drown. Begin when you wish, lady; we'll grant you all the seclusion we may."

Vivayn almost fled to the islet's center, where a dry tussock gave her a place to sit and marshal her powers. At first it was difficult. The daydreams and longings of any girl whose world had been ruthlessly overturned filled her mind with yearnings to escape. If only she could change herself to a swan and fly away, taking her six followers with her, or cause the Jutish boat to break apart, drowning all its rowers, or do any of the things which the ignorant imagined

sorcery made so easy. All she had mastered so far, all she truly had to use, were illusions as fragile as starlight and mist. Her teacher had known how to send the spirit from her body in a different form, to rove freely while the flesh lay inert in a coma, though that was highly perilous. Maybe it was why Gwlythin had not feared death. Conceivably she still lived and had indeed visited Vivayn in that dream. . . .

But Natanleod's daughter had something realistic in her, an invincible preference for what was so, not what she might wish. Her mind listed in a moment all the scores against that comforting supposition. Item: she, Vivayn, had the learned ability to project the visions of her mind. Item: she had done it in her sleep before now, and Gwlythin had cautioned her to learn control over that betraying weakness, lest it bring her shame or worse one day. Item: she had dreamed of the same things Enid and Junius witnessed. The vision of Gwlythin had come from Vivayn's own spirit, giving comfort and advice in the way she could best accept, not from the Otherworld of death. And Vivayn had only that spirit on which she could finally rely.

Tears might have flooded then, but they did not. Vivayn sat breathing slowly until her breath grew tranquil. Then, raising her slim arms, she began to weave magic from the insubstantial air about her, refracting and scattering moonlight across the clear marsh waters.

By morning her preparations were complete, as she had promised. As the first pink of sunrise touched the sky-rim, a strong sea-tide swept in from the direction of the fortress. Something else came across the water with it, a sad, moaning hoot with undertones of defiant hilarity, the cry of a barbarian Jute playing at ghosts to allay his own fears after visiting a place which he believed to be haunted. Raucous voices of his mates joining the game resounded through the dawn.

"Ha ha! They follow us, men — the ghosts of all the slaves whose blood the Roman wizards mixed with mortar to bind their stones together until the world's end! Who will go meet them? You, Oswi?"

"Whooo!"

"We want your heart's gore, Oswi!"

The childish, macabre chorus faded, and an individual voice (Oswi's, no doubt) bellowed in mock wrath: "Let 'em come to me! Let 'em come with their dry veins and I'll pull them out to thong my shoes! All the ghosts who ever died won't stop us from dragging that British witch-girl before Cerdic with her head in a sack!"

Vivayn thought, *That one would make a good companion for our fine Junius. The same empty boasting, and he'd run as far if he ever confronted what he now defies!*

Closing her eyes, she envisioned the complex tapestry of illusion she had woven over the island through a long night. Her mind saw and tallied its every detail.

"Pavilion of air, cover us now until sunset, in the name of Gwydion, master of lore, king of illusion! Baffle the invaders!"

Something like a lace of spiderwebs broke loose from a point above Vivayn's head, to roll downward like a domed tent unfolding over unseen, delicate ribs, spilling down to the shoreline, making a hemisphere of enchanted air about the islet. Vision and light slipped across it, were directed elsewhere, perplexed, mazed, distorted. From within the effect, the seven travellers saw all things as they genuinely were. The creak and splash of oars drew closer.

"Back, you blind worms!" came a yell of near-frenzy. "Back stroke or we'll go aground! Back! Frigg! Could none of you see yonder island? *Back!*"

Vivayn had enough youth left to hug herself in delight. "They've seen an illusion!" she whispered. "A glamor of this isle, perceived where it is not! They could row straight through the mirage if they only knew, for it is a clear channel; but now they must push about looking for another. They will be too weary by nightfall to think of looking for us, or of anything but winning clear of this marsh — and all they will suppose is that they missed their way. It's easy to do."

"You saved us!" Keir whispered back. "I'd never be amazed if they had with them a traitor boatman who does know the place, but small use he'd be to them now — and if he's there, I hope they behead him in disgust!"

Tingling, alight with anticipation, the seven waited while the invaders' boat headed back and forth, impelled by ash oars now employed as poles, to the noise of cursing, advice, and bewildered debate, each suggestion being loudly criticized and sometimes refuted with blows. Vivayn had never prepared so large or complex an illusion before, and took pride in having done it so well. The Jutes were rapidly growing so flustered with anger that they might even turn on each other, when someone shouted, "There! Clear water, dead ahead yonder!"

Catcalls and roars of disbelief welcomed the announcement. The first speaker cried his certainty that he could take their boat through the channel he had espied on any rainy midnight they liked to name, while his mates expressed doubts of it. Finally they agreed to try, on the condition that if he failed they would sacrifice him to their grim gods for a clear passage. He declined the honor and told them to either trust him or find their own way out. Vivayn caught the sense of the words if not their full meaning.

There followed more argument, and finally the boat began to move again, reeds brushing its sides with a rustling whisper as the Jutes thrust it onward. With sudden comprehending horror, Vivayn saw that they were making directly for the islet.

"They are coming here?" Keir asked, puzzled.

"They are!" Vivayn said, appalled. There is land in their way, but they do not see it and they will strike us!" She thought with desperate quickness. "Listen, we must be ready to launch our boat from the isle's far side when they hit; then, perhaps, we can still get away unseen. Keir, do it now, there's no time for talk!"

The warrior gave her one searching look, then nodded and went to do her bidding. The Jutish craft came on, its distinctive high stem-post carved with barbaric designs. Now Vivayn could spit at the bow and hit it, if she felt so inclined. She saw sweat gleaming on the crew's bare arms.

With a glutinous impact, the oncoming vessel struck mud. Driven forward by its own slow momentum, it ran more solidly aground before stopping. Over the creaking and popping of timbers, the curses of frustrated men, and the sucking sounds of oars dragged up from the marsh, Vivayn heard a bear-like bawl issuing orders.

While the Jutes were still confused and noisy, Keir launched his own boat, aided by the other Britons. Poling from the far side of the islet, with all the leafy willows of the place between them and their enemies, they might have disappeared unseen had not Cadaran chosen to play the fool.

"Now, you sea-wolves!" he yelled exultantly. "Tell your master Cerdic the full score of you couldn't catch a few Britons in a leaking punt! Tell him that!"

Keir dealt him a blow that made him stagger and rocked the punt dangerously. "Be quiet, you sheep's-brain!" he barked. In a lower voice he added, "This is no game. If they find us and capture the lady now it will be

your doing. Take your pole and push!"

"Do it if you love me," Vivayn added quickly, as Cadaran looked like making a quarrel of it, his quick Celtic pride aflame after that blow. Hearing, he took his pole again without a word, thrusting in anger so that the punt sped forward over the sleek waters. From behind them came a promise, bawled by the Jutish leader.

"We will follow!"

"Well, there it is," Keir said harshly. "Your joke found a listener, and may you think it worthwhile when one of those Jutish spears rips out your liver. They will follow, just as he said. Push! We have to go by night now, Hol, whatever you say. We cannot stop until next morning, else they will have us."

"With any luck the Jutes will get lost again," Hol grunted.

"With any luck!" Enid echoed bitterly. "We shouldn't be needing more after all that the lady created for us and *you* threw away with your crowing!"

"It wasn't my doing that the Jutes ran aground nigh on top of us!" Cadaran yelled.

"Quiet!" Keir said again. "They will track us with their ears at this rate! No more words!"

"Or I will strike silent the next one to speak when there is no need," Vivayn promised.

Taut with unease and animosity, they poled through the morning while Hol directed them with gestures, guiding them past mud-banks and snags which had the look of monsters waiting to rend. More than once they heard the distant rhythmic chanting of their hunters plying long oars in unison, but they were not acquainted with the marsh, and finding one tiny boat in that expanse of reed was a matter of luck. This time the luck rode with the fugitives whose land it was.

They kept moving for the entire day and night, until the following day they came to the soggy shore of the largest

island they had seen yet. It was almost a third of a mile long. Reed huts upraised on poles allowed its people to sleep in relative dryness, while flat-bottomed craft like their own were moored beneath the floors. The island's level had been raised with layers of brushwood and clay to provide a ground for meetings and ceremonies. Surprisingly, a yard-high stone cross with arms of equal length stood there. Vivayn would have expected a people so isolated and ancient to be heathen still.

Isolated since very ancient times they surely were. Many, including some women, had little hair save thin hanks dangling from the side of their skulls, while their skins were pigmented in variegated patterns which gave them a frog-like appearance. Vivayn realized suddenly that these were Hol's people, and that the patterns on his arms and legs were not peculiar tattoos, as she had always assumed. He'd been born with them. The sight of a naked baby waddling along with rosy markings on its spine and buttocks confirmed her deduction. No child could be tattooed so fully, so young.

"You were born here, Hol!" she said.

"True. They're my mother's people, so I'm one of them by our law of descent. Maybe they'll help us on that account, maybe not. I'll ask, lady — and warn them that sea-wolves are about, too. Let none of you leave the boat until I gain the headman's leave, for it's touchy they are about visitors they never invited."

With that he stepped ashore, displaying his marked limbs to identify himself, while Junius whistled in condescending interest.

"Sa! Now that's about the most words I've heard from him at the one time since I got him to drink a skinful and taught him to sing 'The Mole-Skinner's Wife.' All of it, beginning to end. So these are his people, eh? They have a scent of the Otherworld about 'em to me."

To Vivayn the area smelled of little

save the marsh mud and indifferent sanitation, yet Junius could be right about the dwellers here. They might well have traces of extra-human blood in them. At any rate their squalor did nothing to lessen their health or activeness.

The headman, small and rotund in a kilt which reached his ankles, with kingfisher feathers adorning his sidebraids, came personally to meet Hol. Their colloquy proved impassioned, yet brief, but after inspection of the newcomers as if they were a fisherman's catch, the headman invited them ashore with an expansive gesture. The language he spoke to Hol was completely unknown to Vivayn or any of her companions.

"These are not likely to help us much," Keir said, looking about him. "There are no weapons in this place but bone fish-spears, unless I miss my guess, and twenty Jutes would eat them alive. All they are likely to do is tell our foes which way we have gone."

"Not if they run away first," Vivayn countered, "and they may give us food if we ask them in courtesy. They are not our people, Keir, yet I would not bring them trouble."

Keir's mouth twisted in bitterness. "I'm not so saintly kind! With our kingdom in smoking ruins and our best men slain, it's little to me what may happen to these poor marsh-rats. Their huts must have been burned many times before. They will never lack reeds to rebuild 'em."

"Right you are." Junius leered at a diminutive girl on the shore. "Their women grow old quickly, but they are not bad young, d'you notice?"

"I'll wait until I reach a town of human folk, I think. So should you, unless you want to awaken in the morning to find a hundred years gone by."

Vivayn might have added a more ribald likelihood to Keir's warning, but she felt assailed by grief after his comments concerning the fate of their kingdom. Somewhere to the north her father lay dead, and she was a fugitive among the reeds, helpless even to seek his body and give it proper burial before the carrion birds —

She slew that thought. Most of Vivayn's life had been lived with the barbarian Cerdic for her neighbor across a narrow band of water, and she had seen his henchmen come to Hamo for their yearly tribute; she had known what could happen whenever Cerdic willed it. A bitter hatred had been growing in her heart for the Jutish marauder since the night she had fled her father's town and seen its roofs burning. She hoped he would die miserably when his time came, and that she, Vivayn, would witness it.

That was for a hypothetical future, though. At present they were running from a band of Cerdic's wild pirates and begging the aid of marsh-folk who did not even know the use of metal. She was supposed to be the leader here; in such a situation, what did a leader do? Vivayn supposed that he controlled his own people's behaviour and conferred with the other leader. He showed as brave and prepossessing a face as he — or she — could.

The second part was easy for her. To improve her appearance unobtrusively, one aspect at a time, by the use of illusion, was something Vivayn could do in any spare moment. Thus she stepped ashore with her hair smoothly coiffed, her face immaculate, and a sheen of bluebells on her cloak, despite having fled through the marshes for two days. The tiny glamor lifted her spirits and certainly had its effect upon her followers. Keir commented wryly that the marsh-folk should take her for a goddess now. Enid stammered her admiration while Cadaran, in young bravado, whistled — but the eyes of Junius narrowed beneath the small puckered brand on his forehead, and he watched Vivayn with shifty calculation as she spoke to the headman with Hol for an interpreter. Junius had seen these powers of illusion-casting at work once too often now, and familiarity was breeding contempt. He began to see the ghost which had terrified him as just another trick by a green girl, and resentment surged in his heart. For *that* he had vowed loyalty to her?

Vivayn did not see the big man's expression. Her concern was with the marsh headman, Prasutagh. Exchanging greetings with him through Hol, Vivayn thought that he had the gentlest face she had ever seen, yet two of the shrewdest eyes. Originally prepared to lie a little, she now decided against it.

"We are hunted," she said simply. Hol rendered her words into the ancient marsh language as she spoke. "Twenty men in a great boat follow us. They have iron spears and axes. If they find your village, even by chance, even if you are not here, they will burn it for no better reason than to pass the time, and any they find they will slay. You should prepare to hide."

Prasutagh answered through Hol, "It's no new story. We've had to hide from you dryland lords many times. Now the Jutes come; a new name but the same old tale."

"My father's men never did you harm," Vivayn declared. "My father's law forbade them to molest you. These newcomers are not like that; the birds know it, so why should it be hidden from Prasutagh?"

The daughter of Natanleod need not be afraid for us," came the answer. "We can hide in an hour so that no man can find us, not even a wizard. We knew you were coming, and we will know when the Jutes come. Now. What may we do to aid Vivayn?"

Vivayn's knees began to quiver. She locked them stiff. "We are hungry, and have need of a place to hide if the strangers come."

"That we can give you. What you say of your father is only the truth, and for his sake you shall eat with us, and share our places of refuge. Since these marshes were made we have lived in them, and fled for refuge each generation. We are never found, and nor will you be."

The painful tightness came to Vivayn's throat again. There was no treachery, no guile in the marsh-man's offer. She had to believe; and belief hurt more than being mistrusted or hounded. Savages torched her home, her teacher announced that she was now a disinherited orphan, more savages pursued her night and day, and after all that a half-naked little man with skin patterned like a frog's said, "Welcome. We will help you."

And still she was not set free to weep.

Seated among the small people of the marsh, eating a stew of eels that would have revolted her three days before, Vivayn gave serious thought to the Jutes who hunted her. Their quarry was Vivayn in person; that they all knew beyond any false mercy of a doubt. Cerdic himself wanted her alive and unharmed. Those men would follow her through the rains of the Deluge and the battle-fields of Armageddon for the rewards they had been promised. Her own attempts to elude them had probably failed; if they arrived at Prasutagh's village they would have to be stopped in a more direct way. How that could be done short of physical force, Vivayn did not know, and twenty picked Jutish spearmen possessed more brute force than she and Prasutagh between them could muster.

A little marsh-girl sat beside her, staring at the stranger with a solemn, bi-colored face and finally daring to touch her arm. None reproached her, for in this tribe tiny children were allowed to act much as they wished, short of drowning themselves. The girl seemed fascinated by the white smoothness of Vivayn's skin, caressing it again and again with small fingers, and Vivayn did not mind. It was a pleasant sensation. Of course, beneath the illusion she had cast, that perfect complexion was at present insect-bitten and grimy, but she would restore her appearance to something more true when next she had time to breathe. Taking the child on her knee, Vivayn played with her while finishing the meal, and was rewarded with delighted giggles. The Jutes would amuse themselves by using this mite as a throwing-ball if they came here.

"We must do more than run from them," Vivayn said with determination. "We must stop them! Listen to me, Hol; without their boat they are helpless. Ask Prasutagh if he can destroy it. Then they would have to toil out of this marsh on foot!"

Hol spoke to the Marsh-king in the strange, fluting vocables of their language, and relayed his answer. Vivayn listened with care, for much advice she heard then was outside the range of her short experience. Some, because of Gwlythin's teaching, she would not have previously believed. The white-haired woman, though skilled in her own forms of sorcery, had been narrow-minded concerning all others.

"Prasutagh is willing to help us," Vivayn told her companions. "These people know something of magic too, and between us we can make these swinish pirates cease breathing on our shoulders. I believe him, my friends. By tonight we should have cause to rejoice!"

"That's good hearing, lady," Junius said. His heavy face radiated sincerity.

Enid said querulously, "Rejoice? With all that has befallen? Lady, you would do better to pray for your sire's soul at yonder cross than sit down to brew foul and useless magic with that goblin! What good did it do last time?"

"It kept us all alive and free," Vivayn snapped. "It did more good than your complaints — or Keir's sword, for that matter! If it hasn't set the land free and rebuilt Hamo, that is only because I cannot work miracles!"

"Aye," Keir said. "While I'd like to kill a few Jutes, we all know that if it comes to fighting — now — it will be our last fight. I say we defer that pleasure and trust the lady. Her quick wits got us away from the islet."

Vivayn felt a rush of warmth at his support, but saw with contemporaneous sadness that even Keir was a warrior first. He wished that he had died in battle with his king and could not wait to rectify that lack. What kind of madness made men love the sheen of a polished weapon so well that they ran to war almost from their cradles? Savage and civilized, they all shared it. She liked Prasutagh's ways better.

The meal finished, they climbed to one of the domed reed huts, where appurtenances of primitive magic hung on the walls. Vivayn recognized the cured skins of marsh rats, a fish's skull, net bags holding bunches of herbs and several flint knives, as having purposes arcane rather than homely. Nor did it surprise her that all this existed in the same village as a public cross. Old things always mingled with new; it was the way of life.

They set to work. Prasutagh directed, his weathered, arthritic hands moving in gestures so expressive that Vivayn hardly needed a translation of his words. It reminded her of Hol's way of communicating, not astonishingly, since they belonged to the same people. For Vivayn's part she used her young, nimble, pampered fingers to turn twine, flat reeds, and twigs into an object many a craftsman would have been proud to fashion, with Prasutagh singing over it as she worked. Although she did not understand one word of the song, if his sounds were even truly words, each separate one seemed to burrow and throb in her ears like a live creature.

When they had finished at last, Prasutagh closed his eyes with a sigh.

Watching the shut, heavy lids in their bed of wrinkles, Vivayn wondered if he had fallen asleep from weariness as the aged will. Opening her mouth to question Hol on the matter, she saw him make a gesture cautioning her not to speak. Then it was that Vivayn recognized a wizard's trance, as with her training she should have done instantly, and colored like any other girl of her age.

At last Prasutagh inhaled a bubbling breath and raised his lids. "They come," he said, and Hol scarcely had to translate. "Now we must go."

The entire village piled into the flat-bottomed boats in moments, taking whatever meager possessions they thought worth the trouble and blithely abandoning the rest. They brought their children and their old people aboard as her own folk too often cherished gold, Vivayn noticed, despite the crotchets and complaints of the lone old woman. Then they poled away from shore, to vanish among the rippling miles of rushes like smoke in a heat haze.

"None too soon," Cadaran breathed. "The headman was right, for see! They are coming now."

Out of the blue day appeared the Jutish prow, with overlapping planks sweeping backwards from the stem. When its crew sighted the village, a fierce shout rolled across the water and men rattled their spearheads loudly on shields. Vivayn's mouth felt dry as she approached the shore, nastily aware of what those warriors might do to her if anger and lust proved stronger than memory of their chieftain's orders. She raised the fragile object in her hands, remembering how she had made it with Prasutagh, forcing doubts of its efficacy from her mind.

Rushing from behind her, Junius struck it from her grasp with a force that left her arms numb. As it fell, he seized her with a roar and carried her into the water, splashing forward like a fat seal, laughing over her struggles.

"You can't fool everybody, princess! Now I'll share the reward for you! Ho, you heroes!" he roared to the oncoming Jutes. "Vivayn's here! I have the lady Vivayn, and believe me, I'll drown her if you don't swear by your gods to split with me! What do you say? There must

be one of you who speaks British!"

Vivayn bit him as savagely as she could. Junius dragged her head away, heedless of how his flesh tore between her teeth, and cuffed her semi-conscious. That motion turned him partly towards the shore, whereupon he saw Keir wading out towards him, sword

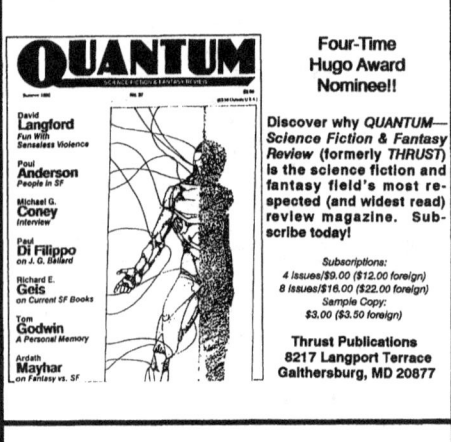
lifted, murder in his eyes. Cadaran was not far behind.

"Oh, no!" Junius called. "Stop there, lads, or she dies and we're all disappointed! I served Natanleod too long to give up my due reward just because the kingdom has changed hands!"

"You fool, no Jute keeps his word! They'll kill you!"

"I'll chance it. Go back!" Junius barked, too short of breath for his usual florid boasts.

The Jutish boat swept closer, and a thrown spear sailed past Keir's dark head, causing him to lower his sword in perplexity. Junius grinned in triumph.

On the shore, Prasutagh bent laboriously down to retrieve what Vivayn had dropped, a reed model of the Jutish boat. Slowly he twisted it in his knuckly, deformed hands until it broke asunder, watching its larger counterpart all the while.

Strakes parted, splitting away from the vessel's ribs, gaps wider than a hand opening in two dozen places. Brackish water poured in, gushing. Men howled in consternation before springing to bail with anything handy, but no efforts could stop their craft filling and settling like a shattered bowl.

Junius's eyes bulged with disbelief as he saw it happen. Keir too was astounded, though in him it mixed with a great and terrible joy. Hurling himself through the water, he slashed at Junius's side with his weapon. The traitor promptly held Vivayn between his own precious body and the blade. Keir, who had expected nothing else from such a dog, and accordingly fooled him with a feint-stroke, now aborted the feint and chopped ruthlessly into Junius's exposed shoulder, giving Vivayn a chance to break free of his weakened grip. Still dazed, she slipped under the water while Junius maintained a frantic clutch on her hair, knowing his captive represented his last slim chance to survive. Keir, equally ruthless in desperation, brought down his blade on Junius's exposed arm, cutting through the muscle. A moment later he was dragging his choking princess shoreward. By the time they reached land she had recovered sufficiently to walk unsupported, although still coughing. Prasutagh welcomed her, his feathers bristling proudly.

"We go now, quickly!" Hol said. "Two boats left, and the Jutes must have none!"

They pushed away from the marge as Junius came staggering over the wet ground, streaming water and gore, clutching his wounded arm. "Lady!" he howled. "Let me go with you — I was possessed by a demon — the Jutes used sorcery on me —"

The Jutes too were floundering ashore by now. They might build a new boat or raft from bundles of reed, in time, but their chance of capturing Vivayn would not return. They would have to vent their frustrations on Junius.

Staring at his agonized face, Vivayn felt a stab of pity, which passed at once when she remembered his gloating laugh as he had offered her to these same Jutes.

"He betrayed you once," Keir said harshly. "He'll do it again."

However, he didn't say no. That decision he left to Vivayn, and he was the man who had risked his own head to rescue her. Keir deserved better than a back-stabbing traitor in the same small boat with him — and so, Vivayn thought proudly, did she.

"There are your friends whom you chose!" she cried. "Ask them for help! By God, it was the like of you who left my father to die without aid!"

Then the dam broke within her at last, and she burst into hurtful, tearing sobs as the boat moved through the water, crying out the last traces of girlhood while Cadaran knelt to ward her with a shield and Keir pushed their boat even faster. Junius yelled promises, threats, pleas, and curses after them in an indiscriminate mixture that made less and less sense the more desperate he became. The last thing they heard of him was a wild shriek of terror as the Jutes closed in, but none of them looked back to see his end.

And the reeds hid both boats from the sight of their baffled foes.

Ω

The Classic Horrors: Cthulhu, drawn by Allen Koszowski "... there is no language for such abysms of shrieking and immemorial lunacy, such eldritch contradictions of all matter, force, and cosmic order. . . . After vigintillions of years . . . loose again, and ravening for delight."
— H.P. Lovecraft

www.ingramcontent.com/pod-product-compliance
Lightning Source LLC
Chambersburg PA
CBHW070601180626
46817CB00005B/1948